Heart of a Lion

Book Two : Langdon Trilogy

By

Susan Elle

For

Ursula Publishing UK

Heart of a Lion

Book Two : Langdon Trilogy

Text Copyright © 2014

By Susan Elle

Ursula Publishing UK

All Rights Reserved.

Cover Photograph

© /Dreamstime.com

ISBN 978-1-910753-22-4

Other Books by Susan Elle

The Sara Colson Trilogy includes
Sara's Child
Sara's Loss
Sara's Shame
All the above also available as audio books.

Catherine Colson-Sayers Investigations
CCS Investigations : Bk 1 : Missing
CCS Investigations : Bk 2 : The Chosen
CCS Investigations : Bk 3 : Travis
CCS Investigations : Bk 4 : Deleted
CCS Investigations : Bk 5 : Mind Games, due out end
Aug 2015, twice the length of previous books.

Tempest
Broken

Love, Lies & Consequences Trilogy
Love : Bk1
Lies : Bk2
Consequences : Bk3

Langdon Trilogy
Heart & Home : Bk1
Heart of a Lion : Bk2
Heart of Stone : Bk3
www.susan-elle.com

TABLE OF CONTENTS

PROLOGUE

Trying to bury myself in work was tiring; exhausting actually, but at least it kept thoughts of Wesley out of my head...most of the time.

I used to live on the family farm, Langdon Farm in Dersley Dale, but now I live in Essex at the riding academy. It was hard, at first – Clara Wentworth, the academy director, had been honest enough to warn me that it would be, first time away from home. She said most of the new starters were homesick for the first few weeks, but that the schedule didn't allow for much wallowing time.

I was glad about that – not only didn't I want to think about how much I missed home I didn't want to have time to think about Wesley Craemer!

Damn the man, it's not like I ever threw myself at him.

The one and only time we ever kissed was when I was 16 – Ronan, my brother's highly strung Arab stallion, ran away with me hanging on for dear life. Nothing I did or said calmed the horse – though I'm sure I would have gotten him under control eventually. Maybe. But, as it happened, I didn't get the chance to find out.

Wesley Craemer, my knight in shining armour, and next door neighbour, jumped on his horse and came charging after us. Wes rode his horse alongside mine, forcing Ronan to veer to the left and eventually into the river that ran through his father's land.

It brought us to a stop alright, but I had been furious, soaked through to the bone in nothing but a t-shirt and jeans.

It wasn't until long afterwards that I really began to understand what had happened that day.

The river had been freezing and I was fighting Wesley off like he had deliberately tried to drown us when, in reality, he'd probably just saved my life.

But at 16 those minor details got lost in the heat of humiliation and fury, and I was suffering both.

My temper has always been quick and hot – I live up to the 'red head' reputation quite admirably, so I'm told.

But I digress – so, I was tussling with Wesley, standing in a freezing cold river and completely unaware of what the water had done to my t-shirt and the nipples that had turned to little pebbles beneath it.

Looking back, I probably could have won a Miss Wet T-shirt competition but, as I said, I was 16 and naïve to boot. I'd had no idea what my body was doing to his while I was thrashing around like that – hell, looking back, I don't think even Wes knew what had happened between us, and maybe that's the crux of the matter.

Ever since he kissed me and put his hands on my body Wes has kept his distance. I don't know if it's embarrassment or disgust that keeps him at such a distance but I miss being friends.

I could always count on Wes to take my side whenever Chad or Matt tried to scold me or ditch me when we were kids. He'd give me a wink and silently mouth where they were going so that I could follow and just mysteriously turn up. Too late then to tell me to go home and, usually, my brother's had grudgingly allowed me to tag along.

Life is very different now, and so am I. At 18 I'm not the naïve teenager I once was. I've had my share of boyfriends, or perhaps I should term them kissing partners as there is never enough time to spend getting to know any of the boys really well or on a regular basis. We're all doing the circuits – a tried and tested round of show-jumping events that take a variety of skill levels to compete in.

You get to know the regulars, but real friendships are hard to form due to the amount of time in between meets. And if, like me, you progress through the ranks to a higher skill level than the person you were friends with, then the types of meets you compete in will differ and so you rarely get to see each other.

It's not as bad as it sounds. I love what I do and so does Fonteyn. She's treated like a queen in the stables and laps up all the attention she gets when we win. She is my one constant, I don't think I would have been able to stay the course if I hadn't been allowed to bring her with me.

CHAPTER ONE

"Alright, Fonteyn, move over – you know the drill," Ashton told the mare as she continued to groom her. "And I know you like to look pretty for the crowd so stop pretending you're not enjoying this."

The piebald mare was fidgety, her muscles almost trembling to get on with the show. She had a competitive spirit and seemed to enjoy the way her rider's fearless heart pushed them both to the limits.

They were a perfect match.

"You got Fonteyn's favourite apples for after the competition?" Katy Forsyth asked on her way to ready her horse for a session with one of the resident coaches.

"Of course." Ashton looked up and gave the young girl a grin then patted her horse lovingly. "She gets her reward win or lose – Fonteyn always gives her best – don't you girl!"

"Gees, you two ought to get married," Katy laughed at her soppy display of affection.

"She's better than any man," Ashton stated, and couldn't help remembering Wesley Craemer. "Aren't you girl," she crooned to Fonteyn after Katy had gone on her way.

The competition was high profile; the academy was expecting great things of Ashton and Fonteyn — there were members of the British Olympic Association expected to be in the audience.

"We usually like to spot our talent earlier in their showjumping careers…" Clara Wentworth had told Ashton on her arrival at the academy, "…but we can't be everywhere at once. You have an excellent track record — your family obviously encouraged your talent; it's just a shame they didn't get you registered for membership of the British Showjumping. We'd have picked you up a lot sooner if they had."

Well, she was here now and was rising fast through the ranks of the showjumping world. Just six months, lots of hard work and a personal coach assigned to her and Ashton was seriously being considered for Team GB under 23's showjumping team.

She had been given a chance that many would envy and only a few ever got — Ashton was part of an elite academy that the richer benefactors of the showjumping world bankrolled. As far as Ashton knew, there wasn't another one like it in the UK, she didn't know if other countries had the same type of facilities.

"Come on, girl, let's go show them how it's done," Ashton crooned in Fonteyn's ear as they entered the competition ring.

As she sat atop her beautifully turned out horse, Ashton tugged on the hem of her riding jacket and straightened her spine – she wanted to win this one very badly.

The audience was rapt, obviously knowledgeable about what they were watching and looked on expectantly as she and Fonteyn readied to begin their round.

Her heart was hammering in her chest; yes, she was nervous, who wouldn't be, but she was excited too. Ashton stilled in her seat, felt Fonteyn still beneath her and knew they were totally in tune with each other.

"This is it, girl, you and me," Ashton whispered, then felt her heart leap as they began their round.

She tried to clear her thoughts, to think of nothing but the next jump, but she had seen him, just before the signal to begin had sounded, she had seen him in the crowd.

Amazingly, and all credit to Fonteyn for carrying her through it, Ashton found that she was half way around the course before she finally focused on the business at hand.

Ok, let's get this done!

They trusted each other, were a partnership like no other, Ashton and Fonteyn flew over fences and made hairpin turns look like child's play...and crossed the finishing line with a very respectable clear round.

"Thanks, girl..." Ashton patted Fonteyn's neck, knowing that it was the mare who had gotten them through it, "...I'll have my mind in the game next time."

"What the hell was that?" Tony Marcella, her coach demanded when she dismounted Fonteyn.

"What...we got a clear round didn't we?!" Ashton defended, but fussed with Fonteyn to hide her embarrassment. Ashton knew what Tony was talking about, she just didn't want to discuss it.

"Because Fonteyn knew what she was doing – where the hell was your head – you looked like your brain was in outer space," Tony snapped.

"Well I'm back on planet earth now," she told him, frowning over Fonteyn's back at the man who had taught her a lot over the last 6 months.

She and Tony had clicked right from the off – she

respected his authority, but more than that, she respected his knowledge. Tony Marcella was one of the best British showjumpers of his time, injury had forced him to give up but he had decided to use his experience to nurture Britain's rising talent – he was also one of the many benefactors of the academy.

"Damn it, Ashton," Tony sighed heavily.

She had the grace to look shame faced as she came round to stand in front of Tony. "Sorry – I thought I saw a familiar face in the crowd, it threw me for a minute."

"Someone from home?"

"Someone from my past."

Tony laughed at that and patted her shoulder, "Ashton, you're not old enough to have a past. Now get your head on straight for the next round."

"Yes boss."

But she couldn't help thinking about the man in the crowd. He'd been standing right in her line of sight – for just a split second she had frozen, her mind so shocked that her thought processes had shut off. But some part of her brain had gone on autopilot, steering Fonteyn round the course relying on the horse to do what she did best.

Hell, I must be cracking up, why would Wesley Craemer be in the crowd? It must have been someone who looked like him, at least enough to make me believe it was him. What a joke – Wesley Craemer here – I must be more tired than I realised!

The second round was tougher, the jumps had been raised. The third round would be tougher still, then they'd be jumping off against the clock.

As she rode into the competition ring for the second time, Ashton couldn't stop her eyes looking for Wesley.

Shit! It is him!

She didn't have time to think anything more before she and Fonteyn were taking the first jump.

Did he have one of his bimbos with him?

The wall was looming large and she steadied Fonteyn, lining her up before they glided safely over it together.

A sharp turn for a tricky double spread – they rattled the first one but took the second one cleanly.

Did he come to watch me?

The water jump posed no problem but the triple caused her some worry. On the middle jump Fonteyn had clipped her rear hooves on the top pole and it had bounced dangerously before settling safely back.

"That's another clear round for Ashton Langdon riding Fonteyn," the disembodied voice announced over the tannoy, and Ashton gave Fonteyn an affectionate slap on the neck as a 'well done'.

"Better, but not by much," Tony told her when she

dismounted Fonteyn again. "You need these points to get you up in the league tables – your past record won't hold any sway with British Showjumping," he reminded her.

Nodding and smiling to placate her coach, Ashton walked off to find the loos.

This was one of the better venues – they had actual plumbed in toilets rather than the often used portaloos.

"Too grand to say hello to your old friends?" Wesley asked as Ashton made to rush by him.

"What...?"

He stood there, tall and lean and looking sinfully handsome with the sun glinting off his shiny blond locks.

"Wesley...I.I didn't see you," Ashton told him, her heart leaping in her chest was beating double time.

His smile was lazy, his eyes assessing as he studied the way she looked in her smart riding outfit. "You running away before the jump-off?"

"Actually, I need the loo," but she hesitated to leave him, somehow unsure and wondering if he'd still be there when she got back – she certainly hoped he would be.

He watched her little jig then chuckled. "Go."

She moved then, dashing into the toilet block and hurriedly spent a penny. Looking in the mirror, Ashton checked her appearance, straightened her clothing and used some water to tame her locks back into place.

What the heck are you doing, Wes isn't interested in you. He's probably got one of his bits of fluff waiting for him somewhere. Urg!

She was scowling when she emerged into the sunshine and Wes was there waiting for her.

"Something happen in there?" he asked, looking past her as if in search of someone.

She actually turned to see who he was looking at then giggled as she realised. "No, no one upset me, I was just thinking...about...things," she told him hesitantly and wished the ground would swallow her up when she felt her cheeks heat up.

He cocked a brow then nodded as if he could read her mind. "I've been thinking about things a lot too lately." He was just about to expand on that when Tony Marcella came out of the crowd looking for Ashton.

With his face creased in concern, Tony's head was turning this way and that until his furious eyes lighted on Ashton. "What the hell...are you trying to ruin your chances...get back here and get yourself ready for the next round!"

Ashton looked suitably chastised and began to walk away when Wes caught her arm. His eyes were blazing as he took in Tony's stance. "Who the hell is that and why is he talking to you like a damned schoolgirl?!"

Putting a hand over Wesley's, Ashton looked up at him and gave a reassuring smile. "That's Tony – he's my coach, and he has a right to be mad. I've not been on my game at all today – I need to go."

With that, Wes let go of her arm and watched as Ashton had it taken by another man, Tony, and he didn't like the look of that at all!

Making his way back to his seat, Wes waited for Ashton to enter the ring on Fonteyn and had to admire the way she looked atop the beautifully groomed horse.

Go get 'em, Ash – show them what you're made of!

He saw her smile as she spotted him in the crowd and he nodded to her in encouragement, returning her smile tenfold.

His heart was in his mouth as she took the first jump and then made an impossible hairpin turn look like a walk in the park as she rounded for the double. They flew over the jumps cleanly and Wes watched her keenly until Ashton and Fonteyn cleared the last fence.

He was pleased to see her search him out, turning to give him a triumphant grin and he stood up, his fist pumping the air above him with a great shout of "Yes!"

Her time was well in front of the other riders, but there were still two more riders to go.

He watched them with mild interest, just wishing they

would get it over with and even wishing the last one would get a fence down when his time looked like beating Ashton's. But he was half a second behind her at the finish and Wes couldn't restrain his broad grin of pride.

The presentation was full of the usual introductions to sponsors and the inevitable speeches, but Wes had his eyes locked on Ashton, his broad chest swelling with pride.

Just look at you, all grown up and looking every bit the champion that you are. Not that you ever had any doubts and neither did I, not really.

He was there when Ashton got back to the horsebox and dismounted Fonteyn. She stood stroking the side of the mare's face for a moment, fondly congratulating the horse for giving another excellent performance.

"I'll get your treat," she told Fonteyn and stepped away to reach for her duffle bag.

"She earned that," Wes smiled, watching as Ashton held a golden delicious apple while Fonteyn chomped away at it.

"She always does – Fonteyn never gives less than her best – do you girl?"

He watched quietly as Ashton continued to fawn over the horse, stroking her gently and kissing the horse's soft muzzle after it had finished eating the apple.

Watching the mare rub the side of her head against Ashton's arm, Wes could have sworn the horse was returning the affection.

"You're quite the team," Wes commented softly.

"Ashton and Fonteyn — we're the best double act on the circuit," Ashton proclaimed with nothing less than absolute certainty. "The rest of the world just doesn't know it yet — but they will."

Wes threw back his head and let out a full bodied laugh at that, watching as Ashton's cheeks flamed.

Then he watched as Tony came over, talking with a couple of smart looking toffs as they walked alongside him.

"Ashton, I want you to meet Bryan Allyn and Ken Follows, representatives of British Showjumping," Tony introduced, standing so as to effectively exclude Wesley from the group.

"Ms Langdon," Bryan Allyn stepped forward, holding out his hand to shake Ashton's. "We've heard good things about you and your performance today was certainly impressive."

"Absolutely," Ken Follows nodded, looking at Ashton down his ski-slope of a nose.

"Thanks," Ashton smiled shyly unable to think of anything else to say.

"As you are no doubt aware, British Showjumping is the governing body of showjumping within Great Britain," Bryan informed Ashton importantly. "I understand you are under the wing of the Equestrienne Academy in Essex," he continued, and nodded at Ashton's muttered 'yes'. "Quite so, an excellent environment for nurturing and supporting our future talent. Good luck to you, Ms Langdon – showjumping is a very competitive sport, but you seem to have the backbone for it, and you've certainly got an excellent coach in Tony," and he turned to smile benevolently at the man to his right.

With that declaration, Bryan Allyn strode off with Ken Follows scuttling quickly after him.

CHAPTER TWO

The moment the two men were out of earshot, Ashton broke into a fit of the giggles.

Wes couldn't help a chuckle and both earned a severe look from Tony Marcella.

"For heaven's sake, Ashton, at least try to look like you respect their opinions," Tony frowned as Ashton tried heroically to rein her laughter in, wiping the back of her hand over her wet eyes.

"I do, I do," she protested, but had to bite down on her bottom lip to stop another bout of the giggles from erupting. Just one look at Wes was her undoing and Tony stormed off when they both doubled up with laughter again.

"I think we just pissed him off," Wes observed when their laughter eventually ceased.

"Tony's alright – he just gets a bit fed up with the fact that I don't stand in awe of the establishment. And why should I..." she added defiantly, "...Fonteyn and I are as good as any of them and a lot better than some!"

"That's my girl," Wes chuckled, loving the defiant fire that flashed in her green eyes. "You never did take crap from anyone."

"It's not that I don't respect them and everything they try to do, but I won't be browbeaten just because I'm not one of the rich and elite," Ashton thrust her chin in the air and turned back to Fonteyn. "We're a great team, aren't we girl?"

Undoing the girth strap, Ashton slid the saddle from Fonteyn's back and rested it atop a fence. Then she got her brushes and, after fetching a bucket of fresh water, began wiping the mare down while she had a refreshing drink.

As he stood back watching her, Wes could see the love that Ashton put into every stroke and felt a pang of ridiculous envy.

As a child, Ashton had looked at him with adoring eyes, a bit of hero worship that had made him feel ten feet tall at times.

That had all changed as they'd entered their teens – like all boys he'd been a bit of a dick, teasing her and razzing her when she did something different with her hair – something 'girly' – but he'd always been fond of Ashton.

And then, of course, there had been that kiss. He'd been 22 at the time and Ashton had been 16 – it had taken him by surprise, the want and desire she'd roused in him, and it had taken all his willpower to pull away and cool off by diving into the cold river.

Jesus! He could feel himself getting hard at the thought of her, remembering Ashton's heated response and the way it had driven him on. He'd lost his head, had taken her nubile breast in his hand and felt the pebble hard nipple push into his palm.

He'd wanted to take it into his mouth, to hear the moan he knew she would let loose at the pleasure he could bring to her, and that had been the instant warning bells had rung in his head.

Pulling his thoughts back with a long sigh, Wes looked at the same girl now and longed to feel her in his arms again.

He'd grown tired of all the nameless bimbo's he'd taken out since that day, determined to keep Ashton at a distance. But as much as he'd ragged on her, Wes had never been able to rid himself of that memory, of the wanting he pushed away whenever he was near her.

She'd been a kid, just a slip of a girl with no experience whatsoever with boys. He doubted she'd ever been kissed before him.

Just look at you now…all legs and curves and lips that a man could lose himself in while kissing you senseless. You're all grown up, just waiting to be awoken by the right man and that man is going to be me!

"Hey, gorgeous!" A young man close to Ashton's age strode over to her with all the airs of a proprietary male. When he pulled Ashton into a clinch and actually put his mouth on hers, Wesley got to his feet and started towards them.

"Hey yourself," Ashton chuckled when they parted. "You didn't ride today – afraid you'd lose to me?" she asked with a wicked glint in her eyes.

"You wish," the young man chuckled. "But I did come to congratulate you. Are you staying overnight this time, or are you heading straight back to Essex?"

Wesley halted his progress, realising that Ashton knew this person better than he liked to think.

"No, we're staying over…" she smiled up at the tall youth, "…Tony's got some business to take care of so-"

Ashton broke off as she remembered Wesley.

He knew he ought to say 'don't mind me, you two enjoy yourselves', but he didn't. He couldn't. The thought of Ashton getting cosy with this other man drove him crazy.

He gave the youth a rueful smile then looked to Ashton and said, "I was hoping to take you out tonight – it's been a while since we caught up – thought you'd like to hear the news from home."

He hadn't needed to cajole – as soon as Ashton heard that he wanted to spend time with her she felt an inner glow that took some hiding.

"Sorry, Josh, maybe next time," she smiled up at him.

"Alright, but I don't think we'll meet up for about a month – I'm taking some time out with my parents, my next meet will be in Birmingham – will you be there?" Josh asked hopefully.

Wesley felt himself tense; if Ashton was planning to go to the meet in Birmingham then he'd make sure that he was there too.

"Yes, so be prepared to take second place," Ashton laughed, then found herself caught up in Josh's arms again.

He was seething by the time the two pulled apart, so much so that Wesley had to turn away and pretend to be looking at Fonteyn.

Coming over to stand beside Wesley, Ashton stroked the side of Fonteyn's neck and then reached for her duffle bag. "You deserve double treats today," she told the horse as she held the sweet apple in her palm for the horse to chomp on. "You're the best."

"Your man there seems to have a bit of a crush on you," Wes observed, purposefully using the diminutive phrasing to undermine the importance of the relationship.

Tilting her head sideways, Ashton thought she must be reading the situation all wrong, Wesley actually sounded jealous. "Josh is 22, I don't think he's had a 'crush' on anyone in a while now. He's really nice," she added when she saw Wesley frown.

"I'm sure he is, especially when he's trying to get into your knickers!"

It was a shocking and unnecessarily hurtful thing to say, but the thought had been voiced before his brain could think better of it.

Her gasp made him turn away, he didn't want to see the hurt in her eyes and know that he had caused it.

"Damn it, Wes, I'm not a little girl anymore!"

He turned then and looked her up and down. "No, you're really not," he capitulated, giving her one of his brightest smiles.

She was hurt and confused; one minute he was good-old-Wes, the boy from back home come for a surprise visit, then he acted like a jealous boyfriend, which was so far out of the realms of possibility that Ashton almost laughed at the thought.

"What's going on, Wes – why are you really here – has something happened back home that I don't know about?" she asked, getting worried now.

Shaking his head, Wes couldn't avoid seeing the hurt and confusion in her eyes now and determined to wipe it all away. "You know me, I'm just being an idiot - I came here to catch up with you. To see my famous friend from the past," he grinned charmingly.

And Ashton was charmed alright. She happily returned his grin then cocked her head to one side and said, "Famous…me?"

"The news is out that you're the golden-girl of showjumping," Wes told her, glad that the tension had gone out of the situation. "Everyone, back home, is following your progress up the league table – they're basking in your reflected glory," he told her, then did a comic bow that made her giggle.

"You're kidding me," she laughed, then looked genuinely shocked when Wes shook his head.

"The Rose & Crown keeps a leader board to track your progress…" he explained, "…and some of the lads have got bets on where you'll be placed come the end of the season."

"Jesus!" Ashton was wide eyed but felt a glow of pride to think of it. "Did you put a bet on me?" she asked.

"Of course – I bet you'd take first place," Wes announced as though there was absolutely no doubt in his mind that she would win his bet for him.

"You are an idiot…" she laughed, feeling a little shy of him, "…I hope you didn't put too much money on me – I don't want to be responsible for you losing your shirt!"

He'd put a hundred pounds on her winning, but he didn't think it would be a good idea to tell Ashton that.

"I think my shirt is in safe hands – just make sure you win or I'll never be able to show my face in the pub again," he chuckled softly.

"We'll give it our best shot, won't we girl," Ashton patted Fonteyn then took some of the hay from the nearby net and wiped her hands with it.

Suddenly the atmosphere changed, a tension that wasn't anything to do with a disagreement sprang up between them and Wes had to push his hands deep into his jeans pocket, to stop them reaching for her.

Before he could say anything, Wes saw Tony striding his way towards them and knew he'd run out of time.

"Have you still got the same mobile number…" he asked quickly, and when she nodded he added, "…good, I'll give you a call to arrange picking you up later."

Then he was gone and Ashton could only look after him. Her heart was still fluttering like it was filled with tiny butterflies when Tony reached her side.

"We need to go over the tapes," her coach told her once he'd got Ashton's attention.

Tony always recorded her when she was competing – he said watching it back helped her to see where she was going wrong or could make improvements.

They climbed into the cab of the large Horsebox and Tony connected the camcorder to his laptop.

She tried, she really did, but Ashton's mind was on Wesley. She spotted him in the crowd at the start of the video – he'd looked proud, she realised as she watched herself and Fonteyn ready themselves to begin the first round.

Tony was pointing at her and Fonteyn on the screen, explaining where he thought they could have done better and how. When she didn't respond to some comment he made, Tony rounded on her sharply.

"You need to get your head out of the clouds – you can't take winning for granted, Ashton," Tony warned sternly. "You have a real talent for showjumping but you won't improve if you don't take notice of what I'm telling you. Now let's go over it again!"

She did listen this time, pushing Wes out of her mind with a determined effort.

Much later, when they had booked into a small hotel and Fonteyn had been bedded down at a friend of Tony's farm for the night, Ashton had a shower and washed her hair, wanting to look her best for Wesley.

She only had a clean pair of jeans and a long emerald green jumper with her, but Ashton left her hair down, the way she knew Wesley liked it, and gave herself an approving nod in the full length bedroom mirror.

She paced the room impatiently, checking her mobile every couple of minutes to make sure she hadn't somehow missed his call.

Then it vibrated in her hand, making her jump, and the sound of her call jingle rent the air on full volume.

"Hello," she spoke quickly into the mobile then sighed when she heard Josh's voice.

Her disappointment must have sounded in her voice because Josh laughed and said, "Not pleased to hear from me – I was hoping your friend had had to go home and I could take you out after-all?"

"Nope, sorry," she chuckled apologetically. "We'll meet up and spend some time together in Birmingham – Wes just wants to catch me up on the news from home."

"Oh really," Josh scoffed disbelieving.

"What do you mean by that?" Ashton snapped at Josh's tone.

"Just that he isn't an elderly uncle — he certainly wasn't looking at you like one, anyway," Josh complained, sounding a little petulant.

"Stop being silly — I've known Wes all my life — he's like a brother to me," Ashton insisted, not convincing Josh or herself.

Any brotherly feelings she'd had for Wes had been banished that day in the river — she hadn't thought of him as a brother for a single moment since that kiss.

"You keep telling yourself that…" Josh pouted over the phone, "…but I'm telling you that he fancies his chances — you just see if I'm right."

A tone on her mobile told Ashton that she had a call waiting and she quickly ended the call with Josh in case it was Wesley and he hung up.

"Hi," she heard Wesley say after she'd picked up the call.

"Hi — sorry about the wait, Josh just called on the off-chance that you couldn't make it tonight," Ashton admitted, feeling suddenly excited and shy at the same time.

"Did he now?"

She thought she detected a note of annoyance and a thrill shivered through her. "Yes, Josh and I have been seeing each other for a while now — he's really very nice."

He'd sounded put out and Ashton decided to play things up a bit to see if she could make Wesley jealous. But her plan backfired when Wes said, "I see, perhaps you would rather go out with him tonight – we can catch up next time you're home."

"No. No," she answered quickly, her heart in her mouth as she feared hearing the line go dead.

"Good," he said eventually. "Tell me where to pick you up and I'll see you in a few minutes."

After giving him the name of the hotel, Ashton again stood in front of the long mirror hung on the back of the bedroom door. I don't even have any make-up with me – he'll look at me and see the kid he knew from back home!

At precisely 7 o'clock, Ashton went down to the small reception area and was pleased to see Wes already waiting for her.

"You look good," he told her when she reached his side. "Where do you fancy going, a restaurant or a pub?"

"I think I'd feel more comfortable in a pub..." Ashton grimaced at her jeans and jumper, "...I didn't know I'd be going out so this is all I have with me."

His smile was brighter than he realised – the knowledge that she hadn't planned to go out with Josh making him feel a whole lot better.

"Pub it is then – I saw a nice one on the way over,"

Wes told her as he put a hand to the small of Ashton's back and guided her out to his car.

She smiled, liking the way it felt to have even that small touch of his hand on her body.

<u>CHAPTER THREE</u>

The pub was lovely and Wes guided Ashton over to a window seat that gave them a view out over a canal. The body of water was dark and still, providing the perfect reflective surface for the bright lights of the pub and nearby street lights.

"It probably doesn't look half as pretty in daylight..." Ashton observed, looking out of the window, "...but it's beautiful right now."

"It certainly is," but Wes was looking at Ashton and not the canal.

Watching his reflection in the window, Ashton could see that he was looking at her and felt her cheeks flush.

Taking her time over the limited menu, Ashton managed to hide herself away until she felt the heat in her cheeks recede.

"I think I'll go for the mixed grill – can't go too far wrong with that," Wes told her as he returned his menu to the small rack.

"Hmm, I quite fancy that myself, just not sure that I should," Ashton smiled ruefully as she looked at Wes over the top of her menu. "Maybe I ought to go for the safe option and order the Caesar salad."

"What do you mean 'safe option'?" Wes frowned across the table at her.

"I can't afford to put on too much weight, it affects my ability in the showjumping arena," Ashton told him quite seriously.

But Wesley waved her excuse away, "What a lot of stuff and nonsense – you've gained a few curves but that's because you're a woman and to be expected. Has that boy been telling you that you're fat – or was it Tony, I wouldn't put it past either of them?!"

"You think I'm fat?" Ashton looked not a little taken aback and more than a little hurt.

Wesley sat up straight in his seat and looked intently across the table at Ashton. "I didn't say you were fat – I asked if Josh or Tony had put that idea in your head." But when she still looked upset, Wes raked his fingers through his hair and said, "Christ, I feel like I just stepped into a minefield – you look absolutely perfect to me, but then you always did!"

Now Ashton looked startled and could only manage a softly spoken, "Oh."

"So, that's two mixed grills?" he asked warily, and let out a sigh of relief when Ashton nodded.

When he rose to go to the bar and order their meal, Ashton watched his progress avidly.

It was daunting to see the attention he got from other women in the pub – one particularly attractive blonde was fairly drooling after him.

But he's with me, she smiled to herself. All mine, even if it's only for a couple of hours.

When he came back, Wes was carrying a pint of lager shandy for himself and a glass of white wine for Ashton.

"Forgot to ask what you wanted – thought I'd be safe with a medium white wine," he smiled hopefully.

"That's great," Ashton told him, trying to be as sophisticated as Wes seemed to expect her to be. In truth, she had never drunk white wine before and didn't touch alcohol at all as a rule. Not that Ashton was averse to it, she just didn't have occasion to drink being so busy at the academy and rarely going out socially.

"Have you spoken to Chad and Matt recently?" Wes asked in conversation.

"Not for a couple of weeks…" she confessed guiltily, "…I tend to lose track of time – the days fly by and before I know it a week has passed."

"Do you miss it?" Wes asked, and watched as Ashton took his meaning without further explanation.

"I'd be lying if I said I didn't – but I do love what I'm doing," Ashton qualified quickly. "It's just…well…I always saw myself on the farm – I miss the animals, the smells, and the open countryside that I could walk in whenever I got a yen. And, of course, I miss my family and friends," she added shyly.

"Good to know," Wes told her and sipped his drink.

"What about Pam, do you two keep in touch?"

Ashton laughed, suddenly relaxed and happy. "Isn't it wonderful about her and Matt – I spoke to her yesterday and she sent me a photo of the engagement ring on my mobile."

Wes grinned, "Damn fool nearly mucked it up, but they were always meant to be, everyone said so."

"Yes, I think mum and dad would have been shocked had he really married Fenella Swain."

Rolling his eyes and shaking his head in despair, Wes said, "That was a narrow escape he had there. Not that Fenella is a bad sort," and he smiled when Ashton grimaced. "She's really quite nice when you get to know her – it's her dad that's on the scary side."

But Ashton didn't understand, she hadn't heard anything bad about Fenella's father, other than he wanted his daughter to marry Matt.

"I know he was a bit over the top with the marriage thing…" Ashton frowned curiously, "…but what makes you think he's scary?"

Shifting in his seat, Wes began to think he'd put his foot in it – perhaps Matt and Chad had kept the details of what had happened away from Ashton deliberately.

"Nothing really," he dismissed with a wave of his hand. "Just wouldn't want him as my father-in-law," and he shuddered dramatically to make his point.

Letting it pass, Ashton gave him the smile he'd been angling for but determined to ask Pam about Fenella's father next chance she got.

Sipping cautiously at her wine, Ashton found she quite liked it and something must have shown on her face.

"You haven't had that before, have you?" Wes asked with a knowing smile.

She wanted to tell him she'd had plenty of wine before and that she often went out to fancy restaurants with Josh or some other boy, but she didn't.

"It never occurred to me," she told him honestly. "I don't have time for restaurants and pubs so drinking never came into my head."

He watched her sip the wine and was pleased that she seemed to like it. "You've lived a sheltered life for all the travelling you've been doing of late."

Lifting her chin, Ashton gave Wes a defiant look that warned him of trouble on the horizon. "I've been to my share of parties…" she told him, "…Dersley Dale isn't as boring as some might think."

Remembering Matt complaining to him about Ashton being a handful, Wes narrowed his eyes at her. "So, you're worldly wise and all grown up," he taunted, not liking the idea of her getting drunk at some party. "Next you'll be telling me you're not a virgin."

Swallowing her wine the wrong way, Ashton coughed and spluttered just as the waitress brought their meals over. She put the plates on the table and patted Ashton's back nervously. "Are you ok – should I get someone?"

But Ashton, red faced and mortified, shook her head. "No, it's ok, I'm fine."

The waitress scuttled quickly away, glad the sudden emergency was over.

"Here, take a sip of this…" Wes offered her his pint of shandy, "…it's more refreshing than wine."

Doing as she was told, Ashton sipped on the shandy until her throat felt soothed. "Thanks," she told him as she handed Wes his drink back.

Lowering her eyes to the plate in front of her, Ashton tried to pretend Wes had never asked such an embarrassing question and picked up her knife and fork.

"So…are you?" Wes persisted, and watched Ashton heave a sigh.

"That is none of your business," she told him boldly, and put a fork full of steak and mushrooms into her mouth.

"It is if I say it is," Wes told her, sounding like Chad when he was determined to get his way. "Now answer the damn question!"

But Ashton remained defiant and silent, eating her meal like they were enjoying a companionable evening together. "This is lovely, you should eat while it's still hot."

"Ashton!" His voice was low and full of threat as he ground out her name.

"No…" she told him, green eyes sparking and her chin thrust out rebelliously, "…no I am not – is that clear enough for you – is that what you wanted to hear?!"

His mouth went dry and he dropped his hands into his lap where they balled into fists. "Who was he – don't tell me it was that jumped up ponce you were talking to today!"

She cocked an eyebrow, as angry as he now. "Who said there has only been one?"

"You-" He broke off, not daring to speak for what he might say. Then he rose, went to the bar and paid their bill. "We're leaving," Wes told her, and stood waiting for Ashton to comply.

But Ashton merely scooped up another forkful of the mixed grill and popped it into her mouth while looking up at him.

His body vibrated with anger, but outwardly he looked still and as rigid as a statue. "Don't push me, Ashton – I'll gladly carry you out of here if that's what it takes," he murmured threateningly.

She knew he could, would if she didn't get to her feet, yet Ashton sat staring up at him daring Wes to try it.

"Fine!" He bent, hauled Ashton off her chair and threw her over his shoulder like a sack of spuds. She kicked and pounded on his back with her fists, and all to the applause of the rest of the patrons.

"Put me down, you great ape!" she bellowed.

"You behave like a child and I'll treat you like one," Wes told her, and didn't set her down until they were back out on the street.

"How dare you!"

"I dare because you taunted me," Wes told her calmly. "Now get in the car, like a good little girl, and I'll take you back to the hotel – you can get a late supper there."

Regretting her actions, Ashton only stared at him. She

didn't want the evening to be over, hadn't wanted it to turn out like this.

"What now?" he asked seeing the confusion on her face, then was shocked to see tears pricking her eyes.

Pulling her into his arms, Wes moved her against him and just held her. "You drive me crazy, you know that don't you?" he told her gently.

He felt her nod silently against his chest as her arms came up to encircle his waist.

They stood like that for a moment or two, just enjoying the closeness and breathing each other in.

"I lied," she mumbled into his shirt, then felt his hands on her arms as Wes held her away from him to look her in the eye.

"You lied…?" He watched her bite her bottom lip and wanted to replace her teeth with his.

Nodding, Ashton's cheeks heated up as she braced to answer his earlier question with more honesty. "I haven't really…you know…"

A smile slid across his lips making him look like the embodiment of sin. Then those lips were coming closer to her own, slowly, giving her the chance to back away if she didn't want this. But Ashton didn't blink, just melted into his arms and moaned when his lips finally closed over hers.

Her head spun — any kissing she had done with the boys she'd gotten to know were as nothing compared to this. Wesley was all man, all heat and muscle that she gladly pressed into and felt the hardening in his jeans.

With great reluctance he pulled away, just enough to come up for air and push back the longing that was burning in his loins.

"I...I don't know what to say," Ashton said breathlessly, and looked up at Wes, her eyes bright with the heat of newly awoken passion.

He considered for a moment, then pulled her back into his arms and laid his cheek on the top of her hair.

"One thing I'd like to hear is that you won't be seeing Josh anymore."

When she hesitated, Wes held his breath then let it out slowly when Ashton nodded. "I'm bound to see him at meets..." she explained, and felt the tension in Wesley as his arms tightened around her, "...but that's all, I promise."

"I tried my damnedest not to let this happen, but you've been in my blood since that day in the river," Wesley admitted ruefully. "I tried to lose myself in other women, told myself the feelings would pass, but you really got under my skin, lady."

She chuckled and lifted her head to look up at him,

"So that's what all the bimbo's were about?"

"You needn't look so damned pleased about it," he chided, but Ashton just continued to grin up at him. "Christ, you're really going to be a pain in my arse, aren't you – you never do as you're told, always dive headlong into danger and constantly put your wellbeing at risk – how the hell am I ever going to sleep at night?"

Now she laughed and threw her head back with glee, "You've always known those things about me – maybe that's why you love me?"

He looked taken aback, then cocked a brow and gave her a lop-sided smile, "And, when did I tell you that?"

Suddenly unsure of herself, Ashton had to think. He hadn't said it, she realised, she had just assumed. But then her chin lifted as another thought entered her head.

"Ah well, if this is just a fling then my promise not to see Josh was given under false pretences…" and she pursed her lips as if giving this thought her full attention. "So maybe-"

Wes cut her off by covering her mouth with his, his lips brutally soft and Ashton had no choice but to give herself up to the kiss.

By the time they drew apart again her head was spinning and Ashton had to hold onto Wes so as not to fall at his feet.

"You were saying...?" His eyes didn't look teasing, they were demanding an answer and Ashton knew better than to lie again.

"Nothing. I gave you my promise, I won't see Josh again," she vowed breathlessly.

His smile softened his eyes and she liked the warmth that came into them. "People say 'I love you' all the time...they don't always mean it," Wes told her, his finger under her chin to hold her gaze. "When I say it I will mean it, and I'll want to hear you say it back to me. For now..." he dipped his head to taste her lips again then smiled like a cat who was tasting the very best cream, "...let's just take our time, get to know each other and enjoy each other's company without putting undue pressure on the relationship. Does that sound ok to you?"

Although she nodded, Ashton frowned, "We grew up together – don't we already know each other enough?"

It was his turn to laugh, and Wes let go of a lot of tension in doing so. "You really are a gem," he told her. "But I'm talking about feelings, emotions - understanding what matters to the other person and learning when to wade in and when to back off – and lots of other stuff that we'll find out about each other along the way."

CHAPTER FOUR

That night, back in her hotel room, Ashton found sleep impossible. Her mind kept going over the way Wes had made her feel, the incredible reality of him wanting her – yes, really wanting her and not just in a physical sense.

She had known that much since the day in the river, even though she hadn't understood fully at the time. And she'd written it off as a one-off aberration that had disgusted Wes and put him off her for life!

Hell, how was I to know what I was doing to him – looking back at it now I was lucky Wes had so much restraint, she recalled vividly. Though I hope he doesn't feel the need to restrain himself for too much longer – I love the way he makes me feel, my body just zings when he touches me – what would it do if he really made love to me?

Thoughts like that kept Ashton awake until the small hours, until her eyelids drooped and dreams took over from thinking. And they were vivid dreams; so vivid that when Ashton woke in the morning she felt all hot and bothered.

"Hell's teeth, this love stuff is exhausting," she told the empty bathroom before stepping under the shower.

Soaping her hands, Ashton smoothed them over her body and became unusually aware of every touch. Her breasts felt full and when her palms skimmed over her nipples they were so sensitive it made her gasp so she did it again.

Closing her eyes, Ashton imagined that the hands roaming over her belonged to Wes and her breathing hitched when they dipped between her thighs.

She whispered his name as a shudder of pleasure ran through her, experiencing her first orgasm.

Good lord, is that what it will be like, she asked herself. Her heart was pounding and took a few moments to calm, as did her breathing. I want him so much – I wonder how long it will be until we're together like that?

Having breakfast with Tony in the hotel was a little embarrassing. It felt like he could see what she was thinking, knew how she had made herself come in the shower and was unusually silent because of it.

"I've never known you this quiet since you came to the academy - what's wrong, that boy giving you trouble?"

She knew he wasn't talking about Josh and felt herself blush. "Wesley is a friend from back home – he isn't giving me any trouble," Ashton stated firmly.

Tony watched her then nodded, seemingly satisfied with her answer. "We'll be leaving in about an hour – got to pick Fonteyn up on the way and then we'll head back to Essex."

"An hour…" Ashton gasped, "…but I thought you said you had some business to do while you were here – isn't that why we stayed over?"

"It is, but I reckon I can get it sorted in an hour if I leave right after breakfast," Tony confirmed.

Now what?! I can't just disappear without seeing Wes – he'll think I've done a runner and changed my mind about being with him," she panicked, her thoughts darting in all directions trying to figure out a solution.

She didn't have his telephone number in her mobile, but he'd called hers on it so, if she was lucky and he hadn't blocked it, she should have it in her call log.

Bolting down the rest of her meal, Ashton excused herself and told Tony that she would be ready to leave when he got back. Then she dashed back up to her room and checked her mobile for Wesley's number.

"Thank heavens," she sighed, and sat on the bed to call Wes.

"Ashton, what's wrong," Wes asked having seen her caller ID on his mobile.

"What makes you think anything is wrong," she replied hesitantly.

"It's 8:15, why else would you be calling so early," Wes told her and waited nervously for her answer.

"We're leaving soon," Ashton sighed sadly. "I was afraid that if I left and we didn't get to say goodbye, or something, you might think I was running out on you."

She heard his smile and felt relief flood through her. "You won't get rid of me that easily," Wes chuckled. "But I would like to see you before you leave – have you had breakfast yet?"

"Just finished – you?"

"I've had coffee, that'll hold me till later," Wes told her. "How about I come and pick you up in say...five minutes?"

Her grin was making her cheeks ache it was so wide. "Great, I'll go down and wait outside."

She took her duffle bag with her – it only held a few toiletries and her jodhpurs, she'd left the rest of her riding gear in the cab of the horsebox.

Standing on the curb, Ashton looked left and right for Wesley's car and hoped that Tony had already left so that he wouldn't see her get in it.

Her wide grin returned and Ashton waved at Wesley's car as it came towards her. When it pulled up to the curb, Ashton climbed into the car and drank Wesley in.

When he smiled and cocked an enquiring brow, Ashton realised that she had been staring and blushed furiously.

Pulling away, Wes asked, "What were you thinking just then?"

Her cheeks felt like they were on fire, but Ashton decided to be honest. "I was just thinking that you're gorgeous and I don't know why you're interested in me," she told him quietly.

Flicking a glance her way, Wes could see that she wasn't joking. "I'm interested in you because you've always been such a great person – one I want to know better and spend a lot of time with."

It made her stomach churn to think he really meant it, but Ashton looked troubled when she lifted her face to look at him. "I want that too..." she assured him, "...but I'm not sure how it will work. I either live in Essex or spend my time travelling to various meets – you live in Dersley Dale and have a farm to run. It isn't going to be easy."

But Wesley wasn't the least bit put out by her gloomy outlook. "I thought about all that before I decided to come here," he told her. "We're just going to have to be patient with each other – there will be times when you can't help but be away and there will be other times when I can't leave the farm – but that doesn't mean it isn't worth pursuing, does it?"

Pulling the car in through the gates of a park, Wesley switched of the engine and turned to look at Ashton.

"Well…?"

Biting on her bottom lip, Ashton considered him then nodded.

"You don't look too happy with that decision," he told her when Ashton still looked troubled.

"No…I am…it's just." She broke off, not sure how to say what she was feeling then just blurted it out. "I don't want you seeing anyone else either. It would break my heart," she admitted softly.

"And you think I will if I have to wait around to see you again," he told her, none too pleased with the idea that Ashton thought him capable of cheating on her. When she didn't reply, Wesley sighed. "I have to admit, the idea of going weeks in between us seeing each other doesn't fill me with joy, but I would never see anyone else while we were still involved."

Her smile was still hesitant and Wesley sighed. "I suppose it's like you said – we have to get to know and trust each other," Ashton reminded him and was pleased when he reached over and took her hand.

"Let's go for a walk and start doing that," he suggested, his hand giving hers a gentle squeeze before letting go.

When they rounded the car and began walking along the path, Ashton beamed up at Wes when he draped an arm over her shoulder and pulled her into his side.

"I have to be back for 9:30 – Tony will kill me if I'm not there when he's ready to leave," Ashton explained.

"I'll make sure you're back on time, but for now we'll just enjoy being together – agreed?"

It was like all her birthdays and Christmas' had arrived together – she, Ashton Langdon, was walking in a park with Wesley Craemer at her side! Amazing!

They walked companionably for a while, then sat on a bench together and reminisced about their shared childhood, the trouble they'd both gotten into along with her brothers and Wesley's sister, Fallon.

"And Pam was no angel…" Ashton recalled, "…I remember her blaming Fallon when she got stuck up a tree and my dad had to get her down – but Fallon had told her not to climb up, she just wanted to do it because me and Fallon were sitting in the tree."

Wesley laughed and hugged her close. "We drove our parents crazy with all the stuff we got up to – especially me Matt and Chad," he admitted. "But that's kids for you – I can't wait until I'm telling my own to 'get down from that tree' or 'keep out of that river'," and Wes chuckled at the picture the thought had painted in his mind.

"Yes, I've always thought 6 was a nice number," Ashton told him, her grin bright and easy.

But Wesley's smile faltered, his expression wary as he looked at her. "Six…you want 6 children?" he asked nonplussed.

She couldn't believe how well she had kept a straight face, but at Wesley's comical expression Ashton fell to pieces. "Gotcha!" she laughed, then screamed when Wes turned and tickled her ribs mercilessly.

"That was cruel," Wes remonstrated, pulling Ashton to her feet to continue their walk.

"But your face was such a picture," she grinned up at him adoringly.

"Hmm, maybe I'll think of something to get you back," Wes told her, but Ashton just tightened her arm around his waist and leaned her head on his chest.

The time to leave came all too soon and they sat looking at each other after pulling up outside of the hotel.

Tony was there putting his things in the cab of the horsebox and when he saw them he frowned disapprovingly.

More than anything, Ashton wanted to lean across the car and kiss Wesley, but Tony kept looking at them.

"This is going to be hell," Wes admitted looking longingly at Ashton, and she nodded in agreement.

"I'd better go before Tony comes and drags me out," Ashton grimaced. "He doesn't look very happy, does he?"

"Don't worry about Tony, he'll soon get used to having me around," Wes smiled encouragingly.

"Will you call me when you get back home?" Ashton asked, already missing him.

"I'll call you tonight around 9," he agreed.

He pulled Ashton towards him and kissed her in spite of the frowning man who was now waiting impatiently behind the wheel of the horsebox.

"That's just so you don't forget me," he smiled.

Climbing out of the car, Ashton felt like her insides were being torn out – she desperately wanted to stay with Wesley.

He watched her climb up into the cab and strap her seatbelt on, then Tony pulled the horsebox away from the curb and Ashton was gone. Jesus, this is going to be agony.

<u>CHAPTER FIVE</u>

Ashton was getting into her riding gear, in less than an hour she would be leaving for the Birmingham show with Tony and Fonteyn.

Braiding her hair, Ashton wound the plait into a bun at the nape of her neck and covered it with a hairnet.

She was excited; after a month of talking to Wesley on her mobile, Ashton was keen to see him in the flesh and reassure herself that they really were an item. It just didn't seem real, at the moment.

Why didn't he tell me any of this when I was home at Christmas – we could have had 2 whole weeks together!

It worried at her, all the time they would spend apart. Wes had always seemed to enjoy the company of women and she wouldn't be around for most of the time.

But Wes had assured her, time and again, that it

wasn't a problem, had said it forced them to take their relationship at a slower pace and that that was a good thing.

She didn't think Wes had sounded very convinced of his own logic and Ashton certainly wasn't convinced.

But today she would see him, would be in Wesley's arms again in a matter of hours.

The journey to Birmingham was long with Tony going over points that he wanted her to remember.

Rolling her eyes, Ashton sighed in exasperation. "Tony, I've got it, you don't need to keep going over it all."

Flicking her a glance, Tony also let go a sigh. "Ashton, you are a terrific rider with a lot of potential, but you need to respect your sport and the other people within it," he told her with great feeling. "It isn't enough just to go hell for leather around a course with no thought for your own safety or that of your horse – one day you could pay a very heavy price!"

She'd heard it all before, but how could she be other than that which she was. It was in her nature to go all out to win – it was in her nature to take risks, to push herself and Fonteyn to the limit – and it was in her nature not to think about the dangers involved, for that would lead to restraint, to doubt, to losing, and that just wasn't Ashton.

Instead of explaining all of that to Tony, Ashton

shrugged and picked up a copy of Horse and Hound and pretended to read.

Tony took the hint and didn't push the issue, but he worried about her all the same.

Wesley found her the moment she arrived and drew her into an embrace even as Tony watched them.

"Christ I've missed you," he told her, not giving Ashton time to reply before claiming her lips in another breath stealing kiss.

"Ashton!" Josh was shocked and unhappy to find her in Wesley's arms, obviously returning his affection.

Pulling quickly apart, Ashton turned to look at Josh and blushed furiously. "Josh, I told you about me and Wesley."

"Yes but I didn't really believe it," Josh stated, his expression one of complete bemusement.

"I'm sorry, Josh. I honestly didn't think you'd be this upset," she told him. But when Ashton made to move towards Josh, she felt Wesley's arm around her waist tighten and stilled.

"Obviously I thought more of you than you did of me," Josh told her then lifted his chin, his eyes going cold. "My mistake!"

"Josh." Ashton called after him as Josh stalked off.

"Let him go," Wes told her, pulling Ashton back into his arms.

"I feel awful – I never meant to hurt him," Ashton moaned into Wesley's chest.

"I can't blame him for falling for you," Wes rocked her as he held Ashton to him.

"Ashton, time to get Fonteyn ready," they heard Tony shout over to them.

"I'll go and get a front row seat," Wesley smiled, and put a gentle hand to her cheek. "No regrets?"

"None," she told him, and knew that it was true.

Of course Ashton wished she hadn't hurt Josh, but she couldn't regret her decision to be with Wes.

"Why are people so complicated," she asked Fonteyn as she tightened the girth and lowered the stirrups on the saddle. "You never let me down or get moody," Ashton crooned, stroking the mare's neck before moving to mount the horse and ready herself for the competition.

She saw Wesley the moment they entered the ring, and Ashton struggled to keep her composure in check. She always wanted to grin like a loon when she looked at Wesley but, for now, Ashton had to channel her focus on Fonteyn and getting a clear round.

There was no need to take unnecessary chances in the first and second round, a clear round was all that was needed. But when it came to riding against the clock, Ashton would pull out all the stops and Fonteyn would give her all that she demanded.

She couldn't resist looking over at Wesley before exiting the ring, her smile of triumph proudly returned.

"That was better," Tony nodded, congratulating Ashton. "Keep that up and we'll be taking home another trophy."

Happy to have pleased Tony, Ashton dismounted and patted Fonteyn fondly.

A short while later, Ashton smiled when she heard over the tannoy that Josh had also achieved a clear round.

"Josh has been on good form, you could end up riding off against him," Tony told her with some concern. "Don't let personal feelings get in the way of doing the job."

"You know me better than that," Ashton frowned. "I can't do anything about hurting Josh – I came here to win and that's what I'm going to do."

The second round was tough, the jumps were not only raised but the spreads were harder to negotiate.

Ashton concentrated like never before, so determined was she to get through to the jump off. She steadied Fonteyn before the double spread, was thrilled when they cleared them both easily. The wall didn't cause either of them a problem and neither did the water jump. The triple was another matter, the spreads were lethal to an unsuspecting rider, but Ashton had gained a lot of crucial experience through the academy and managed another clear round.

She listened intently to the following rounds and smiled when Josh too went clear. Looking over at Tony, Ashton smiled, "Looks like you were right, we will be in the jump-off together."

Wes came round to see Ashton before the jump-off round – like Tony, he was worried about her and Josh going up against each other after their earlier disagreement.

"You feel alright about going up against Josh?"

"Why wouldn't I?" Ashton shrugged her shoulders, pulling her riding hat back on before climbing back up into Fonteyn's saddle. "It's not like I haven't done it before."

"Just stay focused…" Tony warned, "…and don't take any unnecessary risks just to prove a point."

"Will you two stop fretting over me – I'm perfectly capable of thinking for myself!"

With that, Ashton made her way to the ring and awaited her turn. Wesley and Tony exchanged a look then Wes headed back to his seat.

"And now we have Ashton Langdon riding Fonteyn," the tannoy announcer proclaimed.

They walked into the ring, Fonteyn looking beautiful and dignified, Ashton looking ready to do battle.

You've got that daredevil look in your eyes – just take it down a notch and think, damn it!

Their eyes met and Wes did his best to transmit his warning to Ashton in that brief glance, but he was worried.

The starter sounded and Ashton shot forward, Fonteyn responding to her every touch.

Jesus! Wes had his heart in his mouth when they took a tight turn at a dangerous speed and actually rattled the pole on the first fence in the double but it didn't fall.

The crowd were ooing and ahing in shock and relief in turn – and she almost pulled it off.

Just a fraction of a second slower than Josh, Ashton and Fonteyn came in second.

Wesley saw the disappointment on Ashton's face and shot out of his seat to go and offer commiserations.

There were still 3 more riders to go, but it was unlikely that any would beat either Josh or Ashton's time.

He rounded the horsebox in time to see Ashton take off her riding hat and fling it in disgust.

"Hey, hey…" Wes held up a hand of restraint, "…just calm down. You can't expect to win every competition you enter."

Tony came over and echoed his sentiment. "There's no shame in second place, especially with such a respectable time."

But Ashton was furious with herself, knew that she'd allowed doubts to creep in where they hadn't before.

"You two are driving me crazy – you put doubts in my head and I hesitated where I never would have before," Ashton steamed, stalking back and forth, her temper rising. "Why can't you just accept that I am the way I am – going all out is just the way I'm made – I can't do 'careful', that just isn't me!"

"And that kind of attitude is what will get you killed." Tony stood his ground when Ashton whirled on him.

"Just because you got injured doesn't mean that I will," she flung back at him. "I'm more likely to injure myself or Fonteyn if I start doubting myself, hesitating like I did today!"

"Ok. Alright. Christ, I knew you'd be a flaming handful," Wes blew out an exasperated breath. "Can't you just accept that you have people who care about you, who don't want to see you get hurt?!"

"Of course I can accept that – but you have to accept that making me second guess myself is what will put me in danger." Deliberately slowing her breathing, forcing herself to calm down, Ashton looked at both men in turn. "I don't have a death wish, I would never deliberately put myself, or Fonteyn, in harm's way, but I won't compete if I'm not allowed to give it my all," she stated firmly but reasonably. "You know me…" Ashton spoke directly to Wes, "…have known me all of my life. I won't compete with only half my heart – you can't ask that of me."

He wanted, needed, to keep her safe, but Ashton was right. If he tried to change her, tried to curb her natural spirit then he would only succeed in breaking it, and where was the good in that.

Nodding, Wesley walked to her and took Ashton in his arms, gently touching his lips to her forehead. "I hate when you're right – especially when I can't do a thing about it." Touching her cheek with a very gentle hand, he tipped her face up to look at him. "It will tear me apart every time you ride, but that's my worry…not yours. You do what you have to do."

The tannoy announced the prize giving ceremony, and named the winners who needed to come back to the ring.

Reaching up, Ashton placed a kiss on Wesley's lips then turned to smile at Tony.

Retrieving her hat, Ashton dusted it off and mounted Fonteyn. No one would've been able to tell that she had just been bursting with temper and frustration. Her outward appearance was now calm and professional.

Moving quickly, Tony followed Ashton and Wesley returned to his seat at the ring-side.

He was so proud when he saw the way she

congratulated Josh, and noted that the young man was gracious in his acceptance.

Under any other circumstances, Wes was sure he would have liked him, but not while he harboured feelings for Ashton – she was his, now, and Wes was determined to keep it that way.

CHAPTER SIX

Tony had left, taking Fonteyn back to Essex in the horsebox. Ashton was still in Birmingham with Wesley and they were enjoying their time together.

Sitting together at one of the street cafés, Ashton put down her coffee and looked across the small table at Wesley. "I can't believe you talked Tony into letting me go back to the academy with you in the morning – he's usually so strict," Ashton told Wes, sounding incredulous.

"That's because he trusts me," Wes congratulated himself. "He knows I really care about you – I know he cares about you too."

Rolling her eyes at him, Ashton smirked. "Yeah, I've got a real fan-club going on – not!"

Wes smiled, tipping his head to one side, regarding her curiously. "I think Josh was more than a little in love with you – what do you think about that?"

"I think you're crazy is what I think."

"It was nice, the way you congratulated him today."

She looked amazed. "What did you expect me to do, punch his lights out for having the audacity to win?!" Rolling her eyes again, Ashton let out a heavy sigh. "I don't like losing – no one with half an ounce of competitive spirit does – but I don't begrudge someone being better than me on any given day. I'm not a flaming robot."

"No, you're not…" and Wesley chuckled and playfully poked her in the ribs, "…you only wish you were."

But Ashton shook her head, answering him seriously. "It isn't just about winning. Yes, I want to be the best and I want to win because I am the best on that day. But enjoying winning is very different to enjoying beating other people – do you see what I mean?"

He thought about it then nodded. "Yes – some people do enjoy the power trip, the act of defeating their 'enemy' come adversary. But you enjoy the challenge, pushing yourself to the limit and knowing that you rose to the challenge and won. It is different," he conceded.

"That's why I was so angry earlier," Ashton tried to explain. "It wasn't that I was angry at coming second – if I'd given it my best shot then that's just the way it goes sometimes. But I didn't," she told him earnestly, desperate for Wes to understand this important point. "I was distracted, hesitant, second guessing myself and I put Fonteyn at risk by doing so. If she had gotten hurt because of me-"

Her bottom lip trembled and Ashton found herself unable to voice the horrific thought.

"Thankfully neither of you were hurt," Wesley sighed in relief and shuffled his chair to sit closer to Ashton. He put an arm over her shoulders and pulled her into his side. "Not that I'm looking forward to the heart attacks you'll give me every time I watch you ride but, I meant what I said today, you need to ride the way you always have, with guts and instinct and the heart of a lion."

"The heart of a lion...?"

"It's how I think of you – how I've always thought of you," Wesley admitted. "Right back to when you told Chad he wasn't the boss of you and jumped off the swing rope, higher than any of us lads had dared to do, and landed in the swollen river. I about had a heart attack that day, too."

"You're a nervous wreck, Craemer," she laughed up at him.

"You're right – my heart is suffering every which way because of you."

Ashton didn't reply, her eyes were fixed on his, fascinated by the way they appeared to soften yet deepen in colour all at once.

Then his lips were on hers and they both forgot where they were.

A group of lads at nearby tables began cheering when the kiss continued and they broke apart.

Wesley turned to grin at the lads and gave them a salute in recognition.

One of the lads offered some well-meant advice. "Go to it, man, the chic's a babe."

Ashton blushed and Wesley decided it was time to move on. With another casual wave to the now wolf-whistling boys, Wes guided Ashton to a nearby pub.

"Fancy a drink?" Wes asked, while shepherding Ashton to a table.

"Just an Indian Tonic with ice would be nice."

When he returned from the bar, Wesley caught Ashton looking at him under her lashes and wondered what she was thinking.

"You ok?"

She blushed again, giving Wesley an idea of her thoughts. "I just wondered where we're going to sleep tonight – you just told Tony it was taken care of."

"And it is," Wesley confirmed. "I've booked us into a

Holiday Inn – we can go back there after this one and have a drink in the hotel bar.”

Taking a sip of her drink, Ashton tried not to think about the implications of the night ahead, but kept in mind that this is what she has been dreaming about ever since she and Wesley had become an item.

“Can I ask you something?” she looked up at Wes as she placed her drink carefully on the table with unsteady hands.

He cocked a brow and said, “Sure, ask away.”

“What do my brothers know about you and me,” she asked, surprising him. “I mean, do they think you just come to watch me ride – what?”

Wesley shrugged, “I doubt they think anything. I don’t tell Chad or Matt everything I do so if I come to see you it’s my business.”

She gasped. “They don’t know anything – you haven’t even told them that you’re seeing me?!”

Shifting in his seat, Wesley had to think fast. Obviously something had upset Ashton and he just had to work out what.

“I don’t get it, you’re upset that I didn’t discuss our private business with your brothers? Why?”

He watched her stiffen and knew that Ashton was going to get a head of steam up if he didn’t do something.

Holding up a hand he told her, "Just stay calm and explain it to me – do you feel I've done something wrong – should I have asked permission before seeing you?"

Rolling her eyes, Ashton gave Wes a look that told him he hadn't headed her temper off yet!

"I do not need my brothers' permission to see any man I choose," she began, her voice quiet but barely steady. "But I would have thought, seeing as how you've been close friends with both of them all your life, that you would tell them that you're dating their sister! Damn it, Wes, are you ashamed of me?!"

"What?!"

"You heard! Are you ashamed to tell anyone, let alone my brothers, that we are seeing each other?!"

Where the bloody hell did that come from?!

"Tony is well aware that we are 'seeing' each other."

"Don't be obtuse – you know I'm talking about back home," Ashton narrowed her eyes dangerously.

"The only reason I haven't let the cat out of the bag is to protect your privacy – though I can see I should have saved myself the bother."

"Oh really, and how does that work," Ashton asked sceptically.

"Think about it, about who your brothers are. Matt has always been something of a mother hen around you –

which is why it's always been him driving you to horse shows and generally watching over you," Wes began matter of fact. "Then there's Chad – he's always acted like the left hand of God – can you imagine the grilling I'd get after each visit with you?" And Wes gave her a moment to let that sink in. "He'd want to know what we do as well as when and how and how often."

Ashton had the grace to blush at that and sighed. "So you're not ashamed of going out with me?"

Wes took her hand, pulled her closer and gave her a quick kiss on the lips. "Why on earth would I be ashamed – my chick's a babe!"

Laughing at the description the group of wolf-whistling lads had given of her, Ashton finally simmered down. "Sorry, I was being a bit touchy – tell them what you like, or don't, I don't mind."

"Let's just wait until your next home visit then we'll tell them together," Wes smiled, feeling somewhat relieved.

"Well, that gives us a month to get our story straight," Ashton informed him, and smiled when Wes paled. "I'll be home for just over a week at Easter."

They walked to the Holiday Inn, it wasn't far and the evening was balmy.

"Don't you just love clear skies at night...?" Ashton

said, her head tipped back to look at the stars. "It's like looking at a velvet cloth sprinkled with sparkling diamonds."

"Poetically put," Wes smiled and Ashton giggled.

"It was a bit," she grinned. "I must be getting soppy in my old age."

"Soppy can be good – in fact, I think I do soppy pretty well," Wes observed, spinning Ashton into his arms and trapping her against a wall.

The kiss was warm then hot and then Ashton thought she might have steam coming out of her ears. Wesley sure knew how to kiss and she lapped it up and returned as good as she got.

Glad to see that she wasn't the only one panting and heavy lidded when they broke apart, Ashton could only think about going up to their room.

"Maybe we should get that drink at the bar now," Wes suggested.

Her jaw dropped but Ashton didn't stay speechless for long. "Actually, I'd rather not – couldn't we just go straight up and see our room – I've never stayed in a Holiday Inn before," she added lamely.

Wes had already checked in and had their key so they were able to take the lift straight up to their room. He'd booked a small suite with a sitting room, bedroom and bathroom – nothing too swanky but better than average.

He was pleased to see that Ashton thought so. She wandered around, touching the fresh flowers he'd ordered and looking at the tray of hot beverages and small kettle the hotel provided.

"I've never stayed in such a lovely room – we tend to stay at smaller hotels, B&B's mostly," Ashton told him.

By 'we', Wes knew Ashton was talking about her and Tony - when they travelled to a show that was too far away for them to travel back the same day they stayed overnight.

Having carried Ashton's duffle bag on the short walk to the hotel, Wes now put it in the bedroom then came back into the sitting room and took a seat.

Hesitating, Ashton wasn't sure what to do and finally had to admit as much to Wesley.

"Just make yourself comfortable – take a shower, if you want – I just put your bag on the bed and the bathroom is just off the bedroom," he explained.

His overnight bag was already in the bedroom – he'd brought it in when he'd checked in earlier that day and had already used the facilities.

"Oh. Oh, ok," she replied nervously, then took herself off to follow his advice.

By the time Ashton got out of the shower and had

finished titivating in the bathroom, she walked back into the bedroom to find Wesley already in bed.

She immediately flushed bright red and felt gauche and stupid – her nightdress had been bought with this night in mind but Ashton hadn't dared to go for anything too sexy. I couldn't carry sexy seductress off if my life depended on it!

But the emerald green satin nightdress held its own appeal for Wesley. It mirrored in her green eyes, making their colour all the more intense and made her red hair stand out like a flame.

She was beautiful.

"Climb in, you'll freeze standing there," Wes smiled and flipped the corner of the bedclothes back.

Walking around the bed, Ashton climbed in, holding her breath, her heart beating nineteen to the dozen – she didn't think her trembling legs would hold her up for much longer, anyway.

But then she frowned and her hand explored, felt for Wesley. "Where the hell are you," she asked, her frown deepening with confusion.

He was lying right next to her but he was under the top sheet while she found herself lying on top of it - Wes had deliberately tucked it under her pillow.

"I want to spend the night with you in my arms…" Wes

explained, "...to wake up and find you still there. But we won't be making love tonight, Ashton, you're not ready for that yet," he stated firmly.

Ashton sat up like a spring action doll and stared at him. "Are you crazy?! You expect me to spend the night in your bed and not...not...do it," she floundered, all embarrassment fleeing to be replaced by shock.

"You've got it," he smiled, loving the contrariness of her sudden mood changes. Maybe he was perverse, but he liked the unpredictability of Ashton, always had.

"But I...we...why?" she finally asked, pinning him with a look that told Wesley he'd better have a damned good reason for his bizarre behaviour.

"Because I want our first time to be special — I want us to know our hearts and be able to seal our commitment with an act of love — we're not there yet, though I want you badly," Wes told her and held the duvet up to show her the evidence of his words.

Her breath caught and Ashton's eyes rounded in shock as they looked upon the tented sheet under which his erection stood to attention.

"But won't that hurt," she asked, swallowing nervously, unable to take her eyes away from the large bulge in the bed-sheet.

Grinning, Wes dropped the duvet and reached for

Ashton. "It won't be comfortable for a while, but it's worth it. You're worth it."

She lay her head on his chest pillowed by his muscular arm, his other arm holding her close.

"I've never done this before," Ashton confessed, then turned her lips into his chest and kissed him there.

"You told me that," Wesley reminded her.

"No, I mean this," Ashton tried again to explain. "Laying with someone this way, even fully clothed, is intimate – I've never been intimate with anyone before you."

The pleasure her words brought to him caused Wesley's heart to skip a beat and his eyes to fill. Ashton had undone him with her innocence and the gift of it she had made to him.

He tightened his hold on her then placed a kiss atop her hair. "I'm glad – I've never been this intimate with a woman either."

He felt her stiffen, put a finger under Ashton's chin and looked into her doubtful eyes. "What's wrong – what did I say?"

Never knowing when Ashton would 'blow', Wesley knew to be cautious.

"How can you say that – are you trying to tell me that you're still a virgin, because I have a hard time believing that?!"

His smile irked her, but Ashton only narrowed her green eyes.

"No, my darling Ashton, I'm not trying to tell you that," Wesley declared, and bent his head to kiss her lips. "But you can bed a woman without ever being intimate with her – true intimacy involves emotions, tenderness, not just the physical act of mating."

She thought about that for a moment, then smiled.

"Ok, I get that," and Ashton snuggled back against him feeling a thrill of something she didn't yet understand.

He held her that way until they fell asleep and Wesley got his dearest wish when he awoke in the morning. Watching Ashton asleep in his arms, Wes stroked the red hair splayed across his chest and realised that he was irretrievably in love her.

CHAPTER SEVEN

It was tough being at the academy when she wanted so desperately to be with Wesley. Ashton thought about their night together often, marvelling at Wesley's restraint.

But he did that for me, she remembered with pride. He could have taken me and I wouldn't have protested – in fact, I was so up for it I couldn't get to sleep for quite a while. He wasn't the only one who suffered that night!

Grooming Fonteyn had always been a pleasure for Ashton, their bond a deep and abiding one. She loved Fonteyn and felt that affection returned by the mare in so many ways, not least the fact that she trusted her rider implicitly.

"You've never let me down," Ashton told the mare as she brushed her neck. "You never hesitate, have never run out when faced with a fence that other horses have balked at – we make a great team."

The mare snorted and appeared to nod in agreement, which made Ashton laugh.

"I wouldn't be here if it weren't for you," she told the mare, and lay her cheek against Fonteyn's warm neck.

"You're a great rider…" she heard Tony's voice coming from the door of the stall and looked over to smile at him, "…a good horse that you have a bond with helps, but you'd still be a great rider on another horse."

Her brows creased, "Why would you say that – I have no intention of riding any other horse."

"Yes, you do," Tony contradicted her. "As part of your training I want you to start riding one of the academy horses – you need to be able to transfer your riding skills to any horse, not just the one you know."

"Why?" Ashton asked simply, uncomfortable at the thought. It felt like she'd be betraying Fonteyn in some way.

"Because some of the more senior competitions require you to ride your competitor's horse," Tony explained. "You need to get comfortable, confident even, in your ability to demand the same level of commitment from any horse you ride."

She thought about that and had to acknowledge that

it made sense. But Ashton didn't have to like it.

"Do I have to enter those competitions – couldn't we just avoid them?"

"We could…" but Ashton could hear the doubt in Tony's voice and waited for the 'but' she knew was coming, "…but you would never advance beyond the level you're at now. You wouldn't, for instance, ever be considered for the Olympic team."

"But…why?" she asked, her dream of a gold medal slipping away.

"Because you would need to take more than just one horse into the competition. What would you do if Fonteyn turned up lame – you have to have a backup or you'd let the whole team down." Tony tried to make Ashton see the practicalities of what he was saying.

Nodding, Ashton could see the reasoning behind his argument but, again, decided she didn't have to like it.

"Ok, so when do we start?" Her tone was almost belligerent, and Ashton stiffened at Fonteyn's side.

"No time like the present – take Fonteyn out to the small paddock, it's too nice a day to be locked inside." Then Tony was gone and Ashton felt like she had to make things right with Fonteyn.

"I won't enjoy it, not one bit," she told the mare while stroking her neck. "You're my buddy, there'll never be a horse as good as you."

Eventually she had to go in search of Tony to find out which horse he expected her to ride.

When she found him, Ashton gaped then stalked toward Tony who was holding the reins of a 17 hand bay gelding.

"Are you trying to get me killed…" she stormed quietly so as not to startle the horse, "…Vanquish is too temperamental, no one can ride him but you!"

Taking that as a compliment, Tony merely smiled. "Scared?" he asked, challenge in his eyes.

Her chin went up and her spine stiffened, just as Tony had known it would.

"Give me those reins!"

Taking the reins from Tony, Ashton began leading the horse slowly round the stable yard, talking to it and stroking its neck all the time she did so.

She wanted Vanquish to settle with her, become comfortable in a stranger's presence. Walking Vanquish to the training paddock, she introduced the horse to the area where she wanted to ride him and the jumps they would be using.

"Ok boy, I'm ready if you are." So saying, Ashton led Vanquish to the mounting block at the side of the field and used it to gently slide into the saddle.

Tony stood back, watching Ashton's progress and

congratulating her on the respect she showed for the horse.

Taking it slowly, Ashton urged Vanquish into an easy canter and skirted the edge of the field a couple of time.

"Ok boy, here we go." She turned the horse towards a simple jump and he took it easily, even snorted as if to tell her that it had been too easy.

She circled the jumps, getting used to the feel of Vanquish and picked out a spread that would be more challenging.

Riding as if she were passing the fence by, Ashton turned Vanquish, just as she might if she were having to make a sharp turn in a competition, and pointed him at the fence. She felt his muscles bunch, his whole body readying, and he took it with no trouble at all.

Now she didn't bother to circle the fences, but took them at speed as if she were against the clock, Vanquish answering her every demand.

Ashton was thrilled; she'd ridden other horses of course, back home on the farm they'd always had at least three horses, one for each of them, but Vanquish was something else. Something else entirely.

Taking the last fence, Ashton slowly brought the horse to a stop then leaned over his neck to pat him and told him in a whisper how brilliant he was.

"Excellent…" Tony proclaimed happily, walking towards horse and rider, "…you will ride Vanquish every day from now on, even if you only take him for a couple of turns round this paddock." Then Tony smiled, his wise eyes crinkling at the corners," I knew you two would get along – two temperamental souls together."

She raised a brow but didn't contradict him, Ashton knew he was right and eventually shrugged.

Swinging her leg over the back of the horse, Ashton dropped to the ground beside Tony and looked up at him. "Bit of a know-it-all, aren't you." But she tilted her head and gave him a cocky smile, then chuckled when he just nodded in agreement.

Her coaching sessions with Tony became more intense and Ashton felt like she was being prepared for something.

She now rode Vanquish almost as much as she rode Fonteyn, and the two were beginning to get an understanding – most of the time.

Vanquish could still have a strop every now and then, but Ashton figured so did she, so what the hell. She'd ride him flat out for a while, giving him the chance to burn off some energy, then they'd get down to work and reach an understanding.

In time, Vanquish stopped his tantrums and just got

on with the job, as if he had decided that he had tested her enough and found Ashton to be worthy.

Tony watched from the side-lines, made mental notes and stood in as fence builder during their sessions.

It was rare for Ashton and Vanquish to get a fence down, but Tony was building them higher and the spreads wider these days.

"What the hell, they don't have them like that in the competitions," Ashton commented when entering the field for another coaching session.

"They do for the Olympics," Tony told her, and looked at Ashton, asking an unspoken question.

Do you want this? Are you ready to rise to the challenge, to work harder than you ever have before?

"Ok," she murmured, and looked around at the course Tony had built with the help of a couple of workers. "Ok," she said again, and nodded, her green eyes lighting up in acceptance of the challenge.

"Good. Let's get to work!"

Easter was almost here and Ashton and Wesley had been making plans for when she came home. Ashton wanted their first priority to be informing her family, and his, that they were an item, but Wesley wasn't so keen on the idea.

"They'll watch every move we make," he reasoned,

not liking the idea at all. "Right now, they wouldn't question if we just went out riding together, but once they know we're a couple they'll start assuming we're up to something and Chad will give me that glare he does so well."

She chuckled, knowing just the glare Wesley was talking about. "Yes, but you know he doesn't mean it — Chad's a big softie under that grizzly bear demeanour."

"Oh, you think so," Wesley scoffed disbelievingly. "I've seen that grizzly bear take a piece out of someone for getting on the wrong side of him — he'd probably just kill me if he thought I was nailing his sister!"

"Are you scared?" Ashton asked slyly, knowing that Wesley would rise to it.

"Don't talk wet!" Wes declared, just as she'd known he would. "I just don't see the point in riling him when we don't have to — I don't want us to come to blows and Chad might feel he has to defend your honour."

"Defend my honour...huh!" Ashton dismissed with a petulant edge to her voice. "I might just as well be locked up in some ivory tower — my 'honour' appears to be very safe in your hands."

The phone went quiet for a while and Ashton wondered if she'd gone too far.

"That was for you, for us," Wes eventually told her, his

voice soft and loving. He'd had time to come to terms with his feelings for Ashton but he still hadn't told her that he loved her.

It wasn't something he wanted to do over the phone. When he told Ashton he loved her, Wesley wanted to see her response and know she felt the same way about him.

"Sorry." Ashton sighed, knowing she had taken her misery out on Wes. "I'm tired – I'm exhausted actually – but I shouldn't take that out on you. I'm glad you want our first time together to be special. Really," she added when he remained silent.

"Why are you so tired?" he asked deciding to change the subject.

"I'm not sure what's going on, but Tony has me working every single day, even on weekends," Ashton groaned. "And the jumps he has me practicing on are huge – Olympic sized!"

That worried Wes and he told her to be careful. "Don't do anything you're not comfortable with – that other horse you told me about doesn't sound very reliable."

"Oh, Vanquish is alright – he's a bit like Chad, all testy and willful but with the heart of a teddy bear when you know how to handle him."

Wesley wasn't convinced...about her assessment of Vanquish or of Chad.

CHAPTER EIGHT

Leaving Fonteyn behind was hard for Ashton but she knew the mare would be well cared for.

Matt was picking her up from the train station and she couldn't wait to see him. Her family had always been close and Ashton still had bouts of homesickness, more-so now that she and Wesley were seeing each other.

"Hey, Ash!"

She looked around and saw Matt grinning at her, waving her over.

Returning his grin, Ashton ran over and was caught up in a hug as Matt swung her around.

"You don't come home often enough," Matt told her, one arm companionably draped over Ashton's shoulders and carrying her small suitcase in his other hand. "Chad's so boring since he's taken to keeping his own company most of the time – he and Fallon still haven't made up," he informed Ashton with a grimace.

"They need their heads knocking together – anyone can see they're made for each other," Ashton declared.

"I suppose you've got boyfriends queued up round the block," Matt sighed, knowing that his little sister was all grown up.

"I'm not short of male company…" Ashton evaded nicely, "…but, to be honest, I'm too tired to see anyone much at the moment."

"Yes – Mac showed me your last letter – he was a bit concerned about the way the academy is pushing you," Matt frowned down at Ashton, his brown eyes looking worried.

"I was probably just having a good moan," Ashton dismissed as they exited the train station and walked round to where Matt had parked his car. "It's not so bad, just a bit intense at the moment."

Climbing in behind the wheel, Matt turned assessing eyes to look at his sister seated next to him.

"I have to admit, you don't look too bad – nothing a good lie in won't cure anyway." Pulling out into traffic, Matt had to smile, "Although, I'm sure you'll manage to get some socialising done while you're home – just don't go crazy on the booze now that you're old enough to drink it!"

"I don't drink," she told him simply. "Or rarely," Ashton corrected, thinking about the wine she sometimes had when Wesley came to Essex, or met up with her at a show, for a visit

"Good to hear," Matt nodded in approval.

"Have you heard from mum and dad recently?" Ashton asked, realising how much she had missed her family. "I got a letter about two weeks ago, but I haven't heard anything since."

"Hmm, we get the odd phone call – the last one was a couple of days ago – mum and dad are in America now, visiting Graceland," he chuckled.

"That's great, dad always has been an Elvis fan and mum thought he was the best looking man on the planet," Ashton laughed. "Did they mention when they'd be coming home?"

"Not yet – their year isn't up till June – I can't see them coming back before then," Matt told her.

"What a pair! How many parents do you know who just take off for a year to go travelling?"

"It's great, isn't it – and they deserve this chance to see the world, they never took much time off from the farm," Matt recalled.

"Have they settled on a place to buy for when they do come home?"

Since the farm had been handed over to Matt, their parents needed to find a home of their own on their return to Dersley Dale. They had said they didn't intend to return to the farm even though they knew they'd be welcome.

Matt's grin had Ashton frowning at him.

"What?"

"I've got a surprise for them." Matt's grin grew as they pulled onto the road that led to Langdon Farm.

Ashton knew about the housing project Matt had started but hadn't expected the progress she was now witnessing. "Matt, this is amazing!"

He drove along the new road that had been constructed and came to a stop outside of a large bungalow. "What do you think – will they like it?"

They both climbed out of the car and stood in front of a long lawned garden that led up to a cottage bungalow.

"Matt, this is beautiful – did you build it with mum and dad in mind?"

"I did," Matt told her proudly. "I remembered mum ooing and ahing over some cottages when we were little and went on one of our rare holidays. "I had the thatch worked by Seb Browning – he's one of the best in the business and added some unique touches to the design."

"I thought Seb was retired?" Ashton frowned up at Matt as he unlocked the front door.

"He is. But when I told him what I wanted and who it was for, Seb agreed immediately."

"I heard he was soft on mum before she met dad," Ashton recalled, her eyes twinkling mischievously.

"That's right, and Seb certainly put his heart into the design – I've never seen such detail on a thatched roof before."

A sizeable sitting room was on the left of the spacious hallway and Ashton took a step inside. "This is lovely – I can just imagine them in here."

"They've got 3 bedrooms, just in case they have visitors or want the grandchildren to stay over," Matt told her, and got a sidelong questioning look from Ashton.

"No, Pam isn't pregnant – but we do want children, in time," Matt explained.

"Good – I can't wait to be an aunty," Ashton smiled fondly at her brother.

"So, you'll be up for babysitting duties when you're home?" he asked playfully.

"Of course – as long as I can have the requisite boyfriend round for company," Ashton offered, and watched Matt frown. "Kidding!"

They walked through to the kitchen diner – a lovely open plan, spacious arrangement that Ashton thought her mother would love.

"This is amazing," Ashton turned to her brother open mouthed. "Don't tell me you picked out the units and that gorgeous Aga?"

"I'll let that insult pass," he told Ashton airily. "But, as it happens, it was Pam's idea. Not that I'd like to try cooking on it!"

"Mum will love it!"

"Looks damned complicated to me," Matt frowned at the multi oven Aga. "The smaller range we have at the farm is functional enough."

"Men!"

As Matt pulled through the farm gates, Ashton felt a wonderful sense of home settle over her.

"Home…there's nowhere quite like it," she sighed.

"I agree – there's nowhere else I'd rather be."

Going up to her room, Ashton pulled on her riding gear and ran down to the stables. "Hey, Lizzy, how are you?"

"Ashton, I didn't know you were back," Lizzy declared, giving Ashton an excited hug. Then she turned and called for Pam. "Ashton's home," Lizzy grinned at Pam when she emerged from one of the stables.

"Ashton!" Pam hurried over and she too gave the young woman a welcome home hug. "You look like you're ready to get back in the saddle."

"I was hoping to take Symphony out for a while – you don't have a lesson planned do you?" Ashton asked, knowing that the riding school had taken off under Pam's management.

"I do have a small group coming in, but I won't need Symphony for that class," Pam told her. "I only use her for my advanced riders – the ones this morning are juniors…novices."

"Great – I'll get her saddled up!"

They chatted and caught up with all the news - Ashton's progress up the league table and the competitions she'd won, Lizzy's much improved riding and the fact that she is now helping to teach alongside Pam.

"I've taken over the bookkeeping now," Pam tells Ashton as she helps her to mount Symphony. "It's the one part of running the farm that Matt hates!"

"Then you're already a great team – when's the wedding?" Ashton grinned down at Pam and wiggled her eyebrows.

"As it happens, we have set the date," Pam informed her future sister-in-law. "We're hoping your parents will be back in June, but just in case they take a bit more time, we've planned for August. We're going to tell them the next time they phone us."

"About time," Ashton rolled her eyes to the sky then

looked back at Pam. "There were times I wondered if you two would ever get together."

Heaving out a sigh, Pam nodded, "Me too. We weren't very good at telling each other how we felt – at least that has changed for the better."

"I'm glad to hear it. I'll be back this afternoon – I'm going to see the Craemers," Ashton informed Pam and Lizzy, before turning the horse and heading out.

I can't wait to see Wesley. I feel like I'm going to burst with it! Two weeks together…well nearly. We can see each other every day, whenever we want. I think I'm in heaven.

Riding Symphony wasn't the same as riding Fonteyn. For Ashton there was no bond, other than the one any rider has with any horse they ride. She loved Fonteyn, they had been a team since she was just a girl entering her first gymkhana.

Tying the horse's reins to a fence post, Ashton made sure they were left long enough to allow Symphony to graze and drink from the nearby water trough.

"Ashton – how lovely to see you," Mrs Craemer declared, scooping her into a motherly hug. "We've been keeping up with your progress on the showjumping circuit…" the woman told her as she bustled Ashton through to the kitchen, "…and we watched you on the television when you rode at Birmingham recently – such a shame you didn't take first place, I don't know how that boy managed to beat you, I'm sure."

"Josh is an excellent rider…" Ashton began as she entered the kitchen and got a welcoming smile from Fallon, "…he's one of my main rivals."

She was disappointed not to see Wesley, but managed to hide it.

"When did you get home?" Fallon asked.

"Not long ago – I stowed my gear and got changed – I was hoping we could go for a ride together," she lied to cover up the original reason for her visit.

"Did you bring Fonteyn back with you?"

"I wish – but no, she's living it up back in Essex – Tony, my coach, treats her like a queen," Ashton laughed.

"Well, she is rather special," Mrs Craemer chimed in as she put the kettle on. "I don't think I've ever seen a horse like her – so full of courage and you can see that she wants to win as much as you do."

They all chuckled at that, then in walked Wesley and took Ashton's breath away.

"Hey, it's the star of the showjumping world come to see us lowly farmers," and Wes doffed an imaginary hat.

Ashton blushed prettily. "You idiot!"

The Craemers were used to the Langdons and all the

banter they exchanged, but Wesley's mother secretly watched and hoped when she saw how her son looked at Ashton.

"Leave her alone, you big bully," Fallon told her brother, and slapped his thigh as he walked by her. "Ashton came to see me – we're going riding when we've finished our tea."

Lifting a brow, Wesley looked at Ashton then pouted comically. "What, I'm not invited – that's very sexist, you know."

Tilting her head at Ashton, Fallon asked a silent question and received a capitulatory roll of the eyes in answer.

"Ok, bro, you can come too," Fallon smiled up at him.

"Are you sure…I wouldn't want to intrude on some important girl talk," he offered, giving the two young women a cautious glance.

"Oh please!" Ashton punched his arm and watched Wes pull a dramatic injured expression as he put a hand to it. "Since when have you cared about such things?!"

"You wound me," Wesley told her, and rubbed at his arm. "I'm a sensitive soul manfully hiding my feelings away so as not to look a fool."

When she grinned up at him, Ashton couldn't hide the love that shone bright enough for all to see, and a look was exchanged between Fallon and her mother.

"I'll go and get changed," Fallon told them as she took her cup and placed it in the sink.

They didn't appear to have heard her, and Mrs Craemer busied herself to hide her smile.

Sitting at the table, opposite Ashton, Wesley tried not to touch her but wanted to very badly. Even the non-too gentle punch had been a welcome contact. I must be losing my mind! It sure as hell feels like I am!

He watched her, noticed every rise and fall of her perfect breasts as Ashton's breathing became shallow, the pulse in her neck jumping wildly.

He wanted to kiss her there, to feel the heat of her blood beneath his lips then trail them down her body to those luscious breasts.

It was as if he had put the thought into words — Ashton's hand flew up to her neck and she blushed furiously.

"Come on…" he told her, grabbing Ashton's elbow and steering her out of the kitchen, "…I need some air!"

But the second they were out the front door, Wesley took her in his arms and kissed Ashton like a dying man taking his first drink in weeks.

The top of her head flew off, the blood in her veins, hot and pounding, coursed through her vibrating body.

She knew what she wanted, was desperate to feel his hands on her as no other man's ever had been, but Ashton didn't know how to get Wesley to agree.

Oh they kissed, and they had touched very tentatively, but she hadn't yet managed to get Wesley to lose control and take it further.

They quickly pulled apart when they heard Fallon calling goodbye to her mother and Ashton went across to Symphony to hide her flushed cheeks.

"Won't keep you a minute…" Fallon called across to her, "…just going to saddle up."

CHAPTER NINE

The Craemer's farm was small compared to their neighbours, the Langdons, but it was well run and particularly beautiful where the river ran through it.

A huge old oak tree stood like a sentry on its bank, a thick knotted rope still dangling from a solid branch.

"It's so wonderful to be back..." Ashton sighed, breathing the smells of the countryside deep into her lungs, "...there's no place like it."

The three sat astride their horses side by side, with Ashton in the middle of the Craemer siblings.

"But you do like what you're doing?" Fallon asked with a concerned frown.

"Yes, I do. I suppose I just want it all — the excitement of competing and the peace of the farm," Ashton smiled.

"Typical — you want your cake and eat it too," Wesley

pursed his lips on a huffed out breath.

But then, he was no better than Ashton, he realised. He enjoyed watching her compete, the way she came alive and the exultation she couldn't hide when she won – but he, too, wanted her home, wanted to be able to see her as and when, do away with all the waiting and the sad goodbyes.

"Don't you think Ash is entitled to feel homesick?" Fallon turned her frown on her brother and deepened it. "You've never stayed away from the farm for more than a couple of days and you race around the place checking that everything is in order the minute you get back."

In the couple of years since their father had died, Wes and Fallon had taken on most of the running of the farm. Mrs Craemer was still active and did a lot for the village's women's association, but heavy farm work was beyond her physical capabilities.

"Of course she's entitled – but life is full of hard choices – it's up to us to make them and live with the consequences of those decisions," Wes shrugged easily.

Ashton looked over at Wesley with a question in her eyes and watched as he read it there.

When are you going to decide to tell everyone about us, and why won't you make me yours completely?!

"Hmm, very wise I'm sure – not so easy to follow

through on," Fallon dismissed, flicking her leg over the back of her saddle and dropping to the ground in one graceful move. "Come on, let's sit for a while."

Ashton and Wesley looked at each other for a moment then followed suit and moved to sit by the river.

The three friends enjoyed swapping snippets of news — the big investigation into Theodore Swain, how everyone had known he would get off due to all his money and influence. Fallon was a bit more compassionate when it came to Fenella Swain, "She didn't deserve to get dragged into it — after all, you don't get to choose your parents."

"No, and we were lucky enough to get fantastic parents," Ashton declared. "Did she get shunned in the village?"

"Didn't show her face," Fallon told her. "She hasn't had any of her famous parties either."

"Now that is a shame…" Wesley smiled, "…they were damned good — hope she gets around to having another one soon!"

Looking shocked and amazed at her brother's insensitivity, Fallon gave him one of her best disapproving scowls. "After everything she put Matt through, I would hope you would show more loyalty than to accept an invitation from the Swains if one ever did materialise!"

But if she hoped to shame Wesley, Fallon fell far short. "I'm loyal to my friends – Matt knows that – but if Fenella ever gets around to having one of her big parties, of course I will go and Matt wouldn't think any less of me for doing so. There's little enough to do in this village, after all."

Ashton wasn't so sure that Wes had got it right but decided to let brother and sister fight it out without her intervention.

After a few more verbal swipes at each other, Fallon and Wesley let it go and Ashton asked, "What about Camille Parsons, did they ever catch whoever killed her?"

"No," Fallon answered, and cast her brother a resentful look that Ashton caught.

"What's wrong – you look annoyed?"

"I am annoyed, and so are Pam and Lizzy," Fallon informed Ashton. "We've all been told that we can't go anywhere unless we're escorted by either him…" and Fallon jerked a thumb in her brother's direction, "…Matt or Chad! I ask you, how ridiculous can you get?!"

"There's nothing wrong with being careful," Wesley told his sister, then turned his gaze to include Ashton. "The same rules will apply to you while you're home – there's a murderer on the loose, don't fight me on this one, Ashton!"

She had no intention of fighting Wesley on it, and told him so. "You won't find me arguing about it – I like my life and want to live to a ripe old age. Surely you're not seriously put out," Ashton turned to Fallon, her tone questioning the sanity of taking such a stance.

"Huh! Just wait until you want to go into the village or to visit a friend – the men work most of the time so you'll have to plan your schedule around theirs," Fallon sulked.

"I dare say it won't be convenient, but still, it has to be better than getting murdered," Ashton shrugged.

"Sensible woman," Wesley declared, giving his sister a satisfied nod.

"Don't look so smug," Fallon told her brother while getting to her feet. "I'm going back – on my own – you two can just carry on being all agreeable!"

Wes didn't stop his sister from riding off on her own – they were on their own farmland and he hadn't seen any strangers hanging around.

Moving nearer to Ashton, Wesley grinned. "Looks like we get to be on our own for a while – why don't we take advantage of the opportunity?"

He lay down on the grass, pulling Ashton to lay beside him. Then he kissed her, gently at first then lost himself in the feel of her in his arms.

"I could kiss you all day and all night too," he moaned

softly. "You taste…lush…" Wes told her after licking his lips, "…and sweet and sexy as hell – I want to taste ever bit of you then start all over again."

The thought made Ashton shudder in anticipation of what that would be like. She'd imagined Wesley's hands on her and thought she had a good idea what it might feel like, but his mouth…Ashton had never even considered that possibility.

"You look stunned – does the thought of me making love to you scare you so much?"

It took a moment to answer him, her pulses were racing and just breathing was a real effort. "Not entirely," Ashton told him. "In fact…" she blushed and could feel the heat flood her cheeks, "…I wish you would. I want to be yours in every possible way."

Her declaration, made so trustingly, had Wesley groaning as he rolled so that she lay on top of him.

"You're killing me. It's bad enough knowing how much I want you, now, knowing that you want me that way too – hell, I'm going to be living in purgatory!"

Loving the intimacy, the feeling of his muscular body beneath hers, Ashton wriggled up the hard length of him until her face was over Wesley's.

"Serves you right – if I'm going to suffer then so are you," and she lowered her lips to his, kissing Wesley with a new-found confidence.

When his hand moved up her body to cup her breast, Ashton groaned into Wesley's mouth and moved to give him better access.

There was nothing that she wouldn't do for him, or allow him to do to her – only Wesley's deep seated determination to do right by Ashton stopped him from taking her there and then.

The sun shone warm on her back and Ashton desperately wanted to remove a few layers of clothing. But when she reached to undo her buttons, Wesley covered her hand with his own and stopped her.

"Don't – I'm not a saint, Ashton." Wesley sat up, taking Ashton with him so that her knees straddled his hips. His lips found the pulse in her throat and kissed her there.

"What do I have to do to convince you that I'm ready for this?" Ashton was angry now and flung herself off him to lie face down on the cool grass.

Reaching across, Wesley stroked her hair and chuckled softly. "If only it were that easy."

Turning to face him, Ashton asked, "Why isn't it?

"Because I care about you too much to take advantage of what you're offering," Wesley stated simply.

"But you wouldn't be taking advantage of me – I know what I want, life-long commitment or not!"

He frowned at that and drew his hand away. "So you're just happy to get your kicks and move on," he suggested angrily. "How come you didn't ask Josh if you just wanted to lose your virginity?!"

She sat up then, hurt by the accusation. "You're a jerk, Wesley Craemer, and I've got better things to do with my time than listen to you make excuses. Man up – damn it - tell everyone we're an item or we won't be for much longer!"

Wesley wasn't quick enough to stop her vaulting onto Symphony's back and taking off towards home. In fact, he'd barely gotten to his feet and slumped back down to the ground just watching until Ashton was out of sight.

Try to do the right thing and this is the thanks I get! For heaven sakes, can't she see how much easier it would be just to climb into her knickers and be done with it. But she means more to me than a quick roll in the hay – I want more, I want to give her more.

He sat for a while longer, turning it over in his mind and coming up with a conclusion that was going to change both their lives completely.

When she's right she's right – we need to tell our families and sod what any of them say!

Christ-all-bloody-mighty, Chas will pound on me for this and Matt won't stop ragging me about it!

Swinging his long, lean frame up into Titan's saddle, Wesley headed over to the Langdon's farm determined to set things right.

When he rode into the stable yard he didn't see anyone around, but he heard some activity in one of the stables. Dismounting, he tethered Titan to a nearby post and went in search of Ashton.

He found her in the stable where she was taking off Symphony's saddle. Watching as she slid it from the mare's back, Wesley stepped forward and asked, "Can I take that for you?"

Jumping a mile off the floor, Ashton whirled to face him, shock in her wide green eyes. "What the hell – Jesus…you scared me half to death!"

"Not as much as you did me when you took off like that," Wesley told her, looking sad and very apologetic. "But you were right, we need to tell our families and damn the consequences."

He'd barely got the words out before Ashton was in his arms. She'd dropped the saddle and had her arms around Wesley's neck, her mouth pressed to his in a gloriously happy kiss.

"You mean it? You really mean it?"

"I do. All this sneaking around is bloody stupid – and Chad never asked me if he could take my sister out so why should it be any different for us?"

Not sure who he was trying to convince, Wesley held Ashton in his arms and decided that any price was worth paying if it meant she would stay there.

"Come on, let's go up to the house and tell them now," Wesley declared, feeling brave and wanting to act while he did.

If Chad wants a piece of me after we've told him then so be it, but I won't make it easy for him. Ashton is a woman now, able to make her own decisions about who she wants to be with and she wants to be with me!

His smile was suddenly bright and, after putting Symphony's tack away, Wesley proudly walked up to the main house with his arm around Ashton's waist.

<u>CHAPTER TEN</u>

They found Matt in his office, his head buried in paperwork and unaware that they'd walked into his office until Wesley coughed.

"What…huh…" Matt looked and sounded confused as he eyed them. "Sorry, did you say something – I didn't realise you were there."

Wesley smiled but shook his head. "We've got something to tell you, but it would be better if Chad were in on it too."

"He's up stairs," Matt told them, his eyes drifting back to the puzzle of invoices on his desk. "Why don't you stay for dinner, we could talk then, couldn't we?" Matt asked absently.

Ashton looked a little annoyed but nodded and Wesley smiled. "Ok, see you both then."

When they got outside, Wesley put an arm around Ashton's shoulders and pulled her in for a kiss. "We could go and tell my mother and Fallon," he suggested.

That made Ashton beam with happiness – at least there would be someone who knew they were a couple at last. "Can we go now?"

They didn't bother to saddle Symphony back up, instead Ashton rode with Wesley on Titan.

Enjoying sitting in such close proximity to Wesley, Ashton snuggled into his broad chest, one strong arm holding her to him, the other holding Titan's reins.

"I have no idea what my mother will say about this, and Fallon…hell, no one knows what my sister is thinking lately – she's still angry with Chad and takes it out on anyone who'll let her."

Looking up at him, Ashton said, "I feel for her, my brother can be a real idiot at times – he wouldn't be an easy man to love."

"Well, that's as maybe, but Fallon can be a pain too. Best to just let them sort themselves out – we won't let their non-relationship interfere with ours, right?" Wes asked, pulling Titan up in front of the house and waiting for Ashton's reply.

"We won't let anyone interfere with our relationship," Ashton told him firmly. "I want to be honest and open about it, but to be frank…I don't care what anyone says, it's only us that really matters."

Dismounting, they loosely tied Titan's reins to the fence and allowed the horse to graze.

With a hand on the door, Wesley looked down at Ashton and said, "Here we go."

Mrs Craemer had to wipe away tears with her apron after hearing their news and Ashton found herself being hugged so fiercely that she had trouble breathing.

"Have you told your parents?" she asked after letting go of Ashton. "I'll bet they were as thrilled as me."

"No, we haven't told anyone else yet," Wes told his mother. "I mean, it's not like we just got engaged," he added nervously. "We just didn't want to feel like we were sneaking around."

"Oh. Oh." His mother looked from her son to Ashton and realised that she had jumped the gun. "Well…I think that's lovely."

"So where's Fallon – might as well tell her too," Wesley frowned looking at the kitchen door as though his sister might walk through it at any moment.

"Wasn't she with you?" Mrs Craemer asked looking confused.

"Damn it! We had a spat and Fallon took off – she said she was going home!" Wes informed his mother.

There had been a couple of women murdered in nearby villages and the person responsible still hadn't been found. For this reason Wes had insisted that Fallon and his mother be accompanied if they were leaving the farm for any reason.

"Maybe she just went off for a ride by herself," Mrs Craemer suggested hopefully. "You know how Fallon gets – sometimes she just needs a little space to calm down."

"Christ! I'm going to ring Matt, see if she's with Pam."

With that, Wes went into the sitting room with Ashton trailing after him.

Matt answered quickly, obviously still in the office working. "Langdon Farm," he stated brusquely.

"Matt, it's Wes, is Fallon over there?"

"I haven't seen her…" Matt replied distractedly, but then his mind came to attention, "…I thought you'd told her not to go off on her own."

"Fat lot of good that did me! We had a disagreement while out riding and she took off, supposedly to go back home," Wes explained.

"Well then, that's probably where she is," Matt sighed.

"No, she isn't – I'm at the house right now and she isn't," Wes bit out, his annoyance getting the better of him.

"Hell! Look, let me take a walk down to the stables she might be there with Pam and Lizzy – I'll call you back," Matt told his friend and hung up.

As Matt was about to leave the house, Chad came down the stairs and caught his worried expression. "What's wrong – you need help with something?"

"I don't know…maybe," Matt hesitated, not sure if telling Chad that Fallon had gone AWOL was a good idea. But he decided it was better than lying to him and said, "Wes just phoned, Fallon isn't at home and he doesn't know where she is. I'm just going to check that she isn't in the stables with Pam and Lizzy."

He watched his brother's spine go rigid and his face pale then Chad was pulling a jacket on to follow Matt out of the front door.

Pam was giving Lizzy a riding lesson – she was on to small jumps now and doing very well.

The young girl raised a hand and waved happily to the two brothers as they strode towards the paddock but her smile faltered as they drew nearer.

Pam turned to see what it was that had caused the concern on Lizzy's face and watched Matt and Chad as they strode up to the paddock gate.

"Have you seen Fallon?" Chad bit out before Matt could say anything.

"Fallon…why would you think she was here?" Pam asked instead of answering the question.

"Damn it, Pam, just answer the bloody question!"

Matt put a hand on his brother's arm and gave him a warning frown. "Just calm down and we'll get to the bottom of this without upsetting the girls." Then he turned to Pam and said, "Wes just called, he and Fallon had some sort of fallout and now she's missing from the farm – he told her not to go off on her own but…" He lifted his shoulders in a 'who-knows' gesture and let the sentence tail off.

"Well she hasn't been here," Pam told him. "What are you going to do?"

"We're going to find the bloody woman!" Chad snapped. "And when we do I'll wring her pretty neck!"

Pam looked back at Lizzy when the two men left and found her stable hand looking fearful. "Don't worry, Chad's bark is way worse than his bite." I hope. Poor Fallon, if she has left the farm on her own and Chad finds her he'll give her hell for it!

The two brothers got in Chad's car and drove over to the Craemers to offer their assistance.

"Mrs Craemer, Wes…" Chad said on entering the kitchen and only gave his little sister a frown, "…any news?"

"She obviously wasn't at your place then," Wes growled out. "Shit!"

Fallon sipped tea in Fenella's sitting room, listening to the young woman tell her about her recent woes.

"I think dad went a little crazy, obsessing over me marrying Matt, but I don't think he meant any real harm," Fenella explained earnestly. "He's always tried to 'buy' my happiness and I suppose, for a long time, I let him. But I've set him straight on that score and he's promised not to interfere in future."

"And you think he'll stick to that?" Fallon asked, not so sure that a controlling man like Theodore Swain would step aside so easily.

"Yes. Yes I do," Fenella declared, her face so open that Fallon didn't doubt she believed it. "Mum and I haven't seen much of him since all that upheaval — what with the investigation into my father and him having to fight off a take-over bid on the newspaper, he's been spending a lot of time in London."

"I don't suppose the village gossip has been easy for you or your mother to live with, either," Fallon offered sympathetically.

"No. My mother took some time off from her charity work but a group of her co-workers came round to encourage her not to give in to petty rumours — no one that matters believes them anyway, they said."

But Fallon could see that Fenella hadn't had the same support from any of her own friends.

"Doesn't that go for you too?" Fallon asked, placing her empty teacup on a small table.

"It's not the same – I'm not donating time and money to the charities those women work for," Fenella stated, her eyes hardening. "My mother isn't a stupid woman, she knows it's daddy's money they were really after but she chose not to acknowledge that fact and agreed to return."

Nodding in understanding, Fallon thought for a moment. "Today is the first time I've seen you out and about, even if it was only riding along the lane near your house – have you even tried going into the village?"

It tugged at Fallon's heart to see the other woman's lips tremble and tears gather in her eyes, but she said nothing and waited for Fenella to speak.

Shaking her head, Fenella swallowed back the threatening tears and said, "It isn't worth it. I overheard a couple of our workers talking about the village gossip – it was hateful and I don't want to give them the opportunity to sling it my way."

"So you just hide yourself away and have no one but horses for company," Fallon summed up, her lips pursing at the unfairness of the situation. "Whatever your father did or didn't do isn't your fault and it's wrong to hide yourself away – it makes you look like you're guilty of something."

"I wish I had your guts, you'd no doubt tell them to either put a sock in it or go jump off a cliff," Fenella smiled, grateful that her neighbour seemed to be on her side.

For a moment Fallon just sat looking at Fenella wondering what she could do to help, then she got to her feet and waved a hand at Fenella signalling her to do the same.

"Come on, you're coming back to my place – you can't stay cooped up here for the rest of your life!"

"I don't know, Fallon…maybe your family won't want me around," Fenella worried.

But Fallon wasn't taking no for an answer and took the other woman's elbow, steering her out the house to the horses tethered to a nearby fence.

When they rode up to the Craemer's farm house together, Fallon cast a confused look Fenella's way as they both observed a group of men talking animatedly.

Her brother looked seriously anxious and Fallon immediately thought of her mother. Had something happened to her – had she had an accident of some sort?

Nudging her horse forward, Fallon was startled when one of the men looked up and said, "Fuck me, there she is!"

The group of men turned as one, their faces showing confusion, relief and then annoyance. But when she looked from her brother to Matt and then to Chad, Fallon realised that it was she who was in trouble not her mother.

"Where the hell have you been?!" Chad demanded before Wes could get a word out.

Tensing at his angry demeanour, Fallon didn't dismount but sat looking down at Chad her own temper rising. "That is none of your damned business – I don't answer to you, Chadwick Langdon, so leave me the hell alone!"

"Not a chance!" Chad growled, then took Fallon completely by surprise when he reached up and dragged her off the horse. "These men have been taken from their work in order to find you so don't stand there and tell us it's none of our business," Chad warned, his dark eyes boring into her.

She looked around at the group of men and swallowed back the stinging retort that had formed in her head. "I'm so sorry…" Fallon began, moving to look at each man in turn, "…I honestly didn't realise that going to

Fenella's home for a visit would cause you all so much worry – I really am sorry." And turning to look at her brother and Matt, Fallon's expression told them that she meant it.

"I suppose all's-well-that-ends-well," Wesley pursed his lips but his eyes told her that she was forgiven. "Thanks for turning out," he told the men that were now dispersing. "I'll stand each of you a pint when I see you in the pub."

Fenella was still sat on her horse, not sure what to do in the circumstances, but then she watched as one of the men walked towards her.

"You not staying?" Jackson asked when Fenella looked like she would bolt at any moment.

"I.I'm not sure," she admitted, looking down at Jackson then across at the men talking to Fallon then back at Jackson again.

But Jackson just smiled his easy smile and held his arms up to help Fenella down.

She leaned down, put her hands on his broad shoulders and allowed herself to be lifted to the ground. If there was any shouting or arguing going on, Fenella was no longer aware of it – she was completely entranced by the man who was still holding her by the waist.

She had met Jackson before, of course, but then she'd

only had eyes for Matt. Now, as she looked up into Jackson's rugged face, Fenella felt her insides go liquid.

"We were all worried that Fallon had gone off by herself and might have run into the maniac who's offing women for the hell of it," Jackson explained. "He got another one last night – only 15 miles away this time so we know he's still in the area."

He felt a shiver of fear run through Fenella and nodded. "Yes, that's why we told the women not to go off on their own – I think you should take that advice also."

Nodding, Fenella agreed. "I'll do that, and I'll make sure my mother does also," she told him.

Then Fallon was at her side and Jackson let go his hold on her and stepped away. "Damn it, this wasn't the way I wanted to introduce you to my family," Fallon stated, guiding Fenella into the house. "I completely forgot about the veto on lone trips out – I should have told someone where I was going," Fallon conceded.

Mrs Craemer was in the kitchen with Ashton and moved to put the kettle on – something she always did in a crisis. "Would you like some tea?" she asked Fenella, then looked at Fallon and Ashton to include them in the question.

"If you're already making it, but don't trouble just for me," Fenella smiled uncertainly.

"I could do with a strong cup myself," the older woman told her, and continued with the preparations. "I thought my days of worrying over lost children were far behind me, but today has been an eye-opener."

Fallon went to her mother and they embraced tightly. "I'm so sorry – I truly didn't think. But I will in future," she assured her mother.

Wiping at her eyes with her apron, Mrs Craemer went back to making tea and Fallon sat at the kitchen table with Fenella and Ashton.

"I was riding back to the house when I saw Fenella riding along the lane," Fallon began to explain. "I rode over just to say a quick hello and ended up going to Fenella's for a while. I'm really sorry that I worried you," she told her mother again as she set a mug of tea on the table in front of her.

"Not to worry," Mrs Craemer smiled. "Ashton has kept me company while Wesley and the men went off to look for you.

Feeling really bad, Fallon covered her mother's hand with her own as she took a seat at the table beside her, then she looked across at Ashton. "Thanks for that. I feel like a real idiot!"

"No problem, I was still here with Wes when we realised that you hadn't gone straight back home as we'd thought," Ashton told her. "It was a bit scary when no one could remember seeing you for a while."

"It was my fault really," Fenella put in, feeling terribly guilty for all the angst. "I asked Fallon back to my house, it's been a bit lonely since…well…since dad's troubles," she tailed off sadly.

"People can be very judgemental," Mrs Craemer declared. "Try not to let them get you down, dear – they'll have something else to gossip about soon enough."

Feeling sorry for the woman whose father had caused her brother so much trouble came as something of a shock to Ashton. She sat watching Fenella and had to admit, even just to herself, that none of it had really been her fault.

"You know, if you feel like coming over anytime it might be better to call first," Mrs Craemer began with a warm smile. "That way, we can send one of the men to pick you up and make sure you get here and back home safely."

Feeling her bottom lip tremble, Fenella sucked it in and had to swallow down hard on gathering tears. "That's very thoughtful, I'll do that," Fenella said when she'd gotten her emotions in check.

"That goes for me too," Ashton smiled at Fenella. "If you fancy coming over for a visit you only have to call and either me or Jackson will come and get you."

That did it, the damn of tears broke and flooded down Fenella's cheeks, her sobs heart-breaking to hear.

"Now, now…" Mrs Craemer was out of her seat and put a reassuring arm across Fenella's shoulders, "…don't take on so. You don't have to be on your own, you have friends here," the motherly woman told her.

"That's so kind. You're all so kind," Fenella hiccupped and dried her eyes on the tissue Ashton passed her. "It's been awful – I didn't think anyone would want to know me after everything that happened."

<u>CHAPTER ELEVEN</u>

The evening meal with her brothers, Pam, Lizzy and Wes, had Ashton on edge. The conversation was easy, it was nothing for Wes to be sitting at their dinner table, no more so than if she, Matt or Chad had been sat at the Craemer's dinner table, but tonight was different and Ashton knew it.

"Don't you like the paella?" Pam asked when Ashton pushed it around her plate without eating.

"What? Sorry…" Ashton smiled and shook her head, "…I'm just distracted – it's lovely."

Making an effort to put some of the food in her mouth, Ashton watched Wesley talking and laughing with her brothers and wondered if they'd still be so friendly when their news was out.

She helped Pam and Lizzy to dish up desert then sat

looking down at the bowl of apple crumble and custard with no interest what-so-ever.

"You're clearly not into your food tonight," Pam observed quietly. "Want to tell me what's wrong?"

As quiet as Pam had been, Chad still looked up and narrowed his dark eyes at his sister. "Problem?" he asked with a raised brow.

Her eyes flashed to Wesley and Ashton reached for his hand under the table, but she only shook her head.

"As a matter of fact, we have some news," Wesley announced when Ashton didn't speak, and gave her fingers a gentle squeeze. "Ashton and I wanted to let everyone know that we're a couple. We're not engaged or anything..." he added hastily, remembering his mother's reaction when they'd told her the news, "...but we are an item. A very serious item," Wes added, turning to wink and smile at Ashton.

"And how long has this been going on?" Chad asked, his voice soft but as threatening as if he'd just shouted.

Sitting back in his seat, Wes weighed his life-long friend up and decided that complete honesty was called for. "I've been travelling to see Ashton as often as I could over the last few months, but I've known how I felt about her for a lot longer than that," he admitted.

"But you're always arguing," Matt stated, astounded

at the turn of events. "You don't even seem to like each other half the time!"

But Matt frowned, realising that it had been a while since he'd heard them sniping at each other the way they used to and realised what he'd missed.

Wes just grinned at Matt as the penny dropped then turned his attention back to Chad. "You going to give me a hard time over this?" he asked, holding the other man's gaze without blinking.

Whatever Chad decided to say, it would make no difference to Wesley, but he hoped that his friend would at least give him the chance to prove that he was serious about Ashton.

"Depends..." Chad returned the stare with a stony one of his own, "...are you telling me that you're banging my sister?"

"Jesus – that is none of your damn business!" Ashton exclaimed angrily before Wesley could answer.

But the two men continued to eye each other as though she hadn't spoken.

"No, that's not what I'm telling you," Wesley replied, keeping his voice steady. "But I'm not asking your permission to do so either."

Everyone around the dining table waited with bated breath for Chad's response then let out a collective sigh of relief when he smiled.

"Always knew you had a soft spot for her," Chad nodded as if in acceptance. "Just make sure you take care of her or you'll have me to answer to."

"I am not a child…" Ashton declared hotly, "…I can take care of myself!"

"I'll keep her close," Wesley grinned, then tugged on the hand he was holding and moved in for a quick kiss.

"Christ, I hope you two are not going to be lip-locking all over the place now," Matt frowned in disgust.

"No more than you two," Wesley grinned, looking between Matt and Pam. "I've seen you when you think there's no one looking."

Pam reddened but only smiled shyly, not at all put out that she and Matt had been caught out. They were so happy, and once Matt's parents returned they were going to be married.

"It's nice that you're a couple," Lizzy said with a dreamy look in her eyes. "I think it must be lovely to have someone love you in that special way – all warm and cosy like," she smiled, wondering if she would ever be that lucky.

"Your time will come soon enough," Chad warned, frowning at the young girl who was rapidly blossoming into a very attractive young woman.

Pam had altered some of her unwanted clothes to fit

Lizzy - when she had given them to the girl Lizzy had been overwhelmed by the gift, declaring Pam to be the kindest person in the whole world.

It had been humbling to see the young girl's delight with the second hand clothing, and Pam determined to go through her wardrobe back at the cottage, the minute she was able, to find more clothes for Lizzy.

Lizzy had been shy and pathetically thin when she started working in the Langdon Farm stables, now she was filling out in all the right places.

That fact gave Chad pause for thought when he saw the way a few of the delivery men looked at her. Lizzy was still only 16 and Chad would bet his last penny that she had no experience of men.

He felt responsible for Lizzy, and reluctantly admitted that she had sneaked into a corner of his heart reserved for family. She was like a little sister and, as such, would do as she was damned well told and he would knock seven bells out of any man that touched her!

When Wes and Ashton went for a stroll after the meal and the clearing away was finished, Chad saw the way Lizzy looked after them a dreamy smile on her face.

"You don't seem to be as homesick as you once were, Lizzy," he told the girl when she turned from the sitting room window.

Her smile was bright as she took a seat on the settee and looked across at Chad. "I love it here – the fact that I get paid to do something I love is amazing," she chuckled and got a rare smile from Chad. "And it's better now that I can visit my mum and the kids – Jackson's been great about taking me."

Nodding, Chad could see that Lizzy was happy, genuinely settled into farm life. "Good – just see that you don't go out on your own when you're staying at your mum's. I hope your mother is taking care to do the same."

Shifting in her seat, Lizzy felt guilty that she sometimes disobeyed this directive, as she had to help her mother when needed. "Mum's careful," is all she said.

Not sure why that answer made him feel wary, Chad dismissed it as an overreaction. "Ok then."

Pam and Matt joined them in the sitting room and the conversation became more general.

Outside, Wes and Ashton took a seat amongst the hay bales and looked out of the barn to the midnight sky sprinkled with diamond bright stars.

"I'm so happy now that we're not hiding the way we feel," Ashton told Wes as she rested her head on his shoulder. "Not that I wasn't scared to death when the moment came to tell Chad but he took it well, don't you think?"

A lazy smile tugged at Wesley's gentle lips as he kissed the top of her head. "Chad's always been the observant sort, I think he already had an idea."

Ashton shot her head up to look at Wes in amazement. "You think?"

Chuckling softly, Wes put his lips to her open mouth and took full advantage of the situation. When he lifted his head his hot eyes were enough to melt the parts the passionate kiss hadn't already shot to pieces.

"It wouldn't have made any difference to us whatever Chad might have said, but I think the fact that he said very little was telling."

"Yes…" Ashton sighed and leaned into her man, "…if it had come as a complete shock Chad might have gone all alpha male on us – I'm just glad he didn't."

"Yes, he's as alpha as it gets when it comes to his family," Wes agreed with another chuckle. "Did you see the way he reacted to Lizzy – she's his now, too."

"Chad can be an overbearing son-of-a-bitch, but he truly cares about us all," Ashton conceded. "I know he felt like he'd let dad down when he gave up the farm – but Matt has always been the one who loved Langdon Farm as a farmer needs to, Chad was just better at running it."

"You can say that again," Wes heaved a sigh. "That trouble with Swain had us all worried, but Matt seems to be handling things better since he and Pam finally got it together."

"Too right," Ashton agreed. "But then you know what they say – behind every good man is a brilliant woman."

Wes laughed at her version of the saying and gave her a playful dig in the ribs. "I don't think that's quite how it goes but I get your drift."

Suddenly the laughter left him as he looked down at Ashton now laying back on the hay smiling up at him. But her smile faded as she saw his expression change.

"What's wrong?"

He just shook his head, closed his eyes for a moment then pulled Ashton up and held her in his arms.

Struggling with his emotions, Wesley just held on tight – he'd sworn to himself that he wouldn't tell Ashton he loved her until he knew in his heart that they were a forever couple, but the strain of holding it in was sometimes almost unbearable.

She was so young, so beautiful and so full of life – what if that life took a new direction, what if her showjumping career took her on to bigger and better things, made her want all that such a life could give her?

He couldn't match that, couldn't offer the excitement and challenge that such a life would hold. He was a farmer – right down to the core of his being, Wesley Craemer was a man of the land. He could no more give up the farm than Ashton could give up her showjumping career, and he didn't have the right to ask that of her.

So he would wait, would keep his growing love for Ashton locked away in his heart until...

He didn't know what he was waiting for – a bloody miracle would be needed to fix the disparity of their lifestyles. And that only made him feel all the more guilty, that he wanted Ashton to choose him over her blossoming career.

"I think it just hit me, you're mine now and everyone knows it."

His lips were gentle when they closed over Ashton's and his heart cried out as he held her.

CHAPTER TWELVE

News of another woman's body found had everyone looking over their shoulders.

Men didn't let their wives or daughters out without them, or arranged for the women to go about in groups. School runs now included collective trips to the village shops to minimise the time women spent out of their homes, putting them at risk.

Chad called everyone into the main sitting room, determined to make sure that no one in his care would fall victim to the madman.

"I've been contacted by Baxter, the PI still in my employ," Chad informed them all without preamble. "He told me that a woman's body has been found in Gables Wood – the same person is suspected of killing her as the other three women."

He looked from Ashton to Pam and then to Lizzy. "None of you is to wander off on your own, not even on the farm," he declared sternly.

"But that's ridiculous," Ashton gasped outraged.

Narrowing his eyes at her, Chad's sudden anger all but lasered through Ashton. "Don't give me any grief on this," he demanded hotly. "This farm has hundreds of acres of land that a madman like that can hide in – I'll be contacting Wes to make sure he's with you when you're not with someone here on the farm!"

He watched his sister bristle with anger but was grateful when she didn't voice it.

Now, turning to Pam and Lizzy, he laid out more rules. "No more working separately. Stable work will be done together, riding lessons will be given with both of you in the paddock, and neither of you is to put yourselves at risk at any time – is that understood?!"

Both women nodded obediently and Chad turned his attention to the men. "Work still has to carry on, I understand that, but we'll all need to keep our eyes peeled for signs of strangers in our midst. Jackson..." Chad looked at the sturdy man who had proved his worth in many ways since coming to work with his father on the farm, "...I want you to check the outbuildings daily – twice a day if you can manage it. Look for any signs of someone sleeping there, or anything out of the ordinary and report any findings back to me or Matt – don't try challenging anyone you might come across on your own. This bastard has already taken four lives, let's not give him the chance to up that total."

"I'll make sure it gets done," Jackson nodded. "And I'll check the old Mason place – there's still enough of it standing for someone to use as a temporary shelter."

Over the years, Langdon Farm had grown by acquiring other farms adjoined to it as they became available. The Mason farm had been the last to be added and the old farmhouse had been used for storage until recently. Now it was falling to pieces and complete demolition was scheduled to begin later in the year, but until then it stood eerily empty and alone.

"Good man!"

Life in Dersley Dale was no longer easy going, sociable and welcoming. Women looked at men they had known for years with eyes filled with suspicion and wariness. Somewhere in their midst a murderer lurked, and there was no saying he didn't live in the picturesque village.

Gables Wood stood on the outskirts of the village, it felt like the murderer was working his way towards them and he was taking less time between kills.

The local park looked desolate, no longer alive with

the sound of children having fun and running off steam. The swings only moved if a strong wind blew them and the roundabout and slide were redundant reminders of happier times.

Dersley Dale was waiting, still with anxiety and anticipation, a dark shadow looming large over it.

When it came time for Ashton to return to the riding academy, it was almost a relief.

Wesley drove her instead of allowing Ashton to get the train, giving them a little longer to be together.

"The murdering bastard isn't going to get me while I'm on a train," she had protested when Wes had insisted on driving her all the way to Essex.

Now she was glad he hadn't listened to her and rested back for the long journey.

"At least you're staying overnight — it would be ludicrous for you to try driving to Essex and back in the same day," Ashton observed casually.

"True. But my main reason for staying is to spend some time together tomorrow — it's going to be a while till we see each other after this," Wes frowned, anticipating the agony of the forced separation.

"Sorry," Ashton told him simply. "If it's any consolation, I'll miss you a whole lot more than you'll miss me. I love you, Wesley."

All at once his heart sang with the hope and happiness that her words gave him, but Wesley didn't return the sentiment. Instead he took her hand raised it to his lips then lowered it, keeping their fingers entwined as they continued along the motorway.

It hurt that he didn't say it back. It hurt and it confused Ashton as everything Wesley said or did seemed to tell her that she meant an awful lot to him.

But was it enough, was she enough to hold him and capture his heart completely?

Those thoughts tugged at her, tore at her as they neared the academy and the time when he would leave her again.

But that was her choice, wasn't it? Wesley wasn't leaving her, she was leaving him she realised.

This is crazy – I'm going crazy! How can I be happy doing what I'm doing if it's always going to take me away from the man I love? And worse, what if that's the reason he won't commit – maybe he thinks I'll leave him for good one day, take off with someone I meet along the way and leave him behind without a backward glance?

Well that's just stupid! Surely he knows me better than that – he's known me all my life, for christ's sake! And if he really thinks I'm that shallow, why the hell is he with me in the first place?!

She looked out of the side window, saw blue skies over green fields in a blur as they passed by, and sighed heavily. The weight in her heart grew with every mile they travelled – he would be leaving her soon and it was her fault, her choice.

The first thing she did when they reached the academy was take Wes out to the stables to see Fonteyn.

"Hey girl," she crooned, and the mare snickered happily, nudging her head up and down Ashton's arm. "Did you miss me? I brought you a treat."

She held an apple in the palm of her hand while Fonteyn chomped on it and grinned up at Wesley.

"Would you mind if I took her out for a while?" she asked. "It seems like forever since I've ridden her."

Wesley gave her an indulgent smile and said, "I'm surprised you bothered to ask – I didn't expect you to see Fonteyn and not want to ride her."

She was graceful, full of poise and confidence and Ashton glowed with happiness as she and Fonteyn flew over jump after jump in the training paddock.

This is where you belong, Wesley thought as he watched her. This is where your heart is and where it will always be. Maybe if I wait, let you do what you need to do, you'll find room in your life to settle with me...settle for me.

It hurt to watch her, to see the elation on Ashton's face and the joy so evident in her every move. Fonteyn responded to Ashton almost without her asking, twisting, turning, jumping and trusting her rider without hesitation.

They were poetry in motion, joined in heart, mind and spirit, he could see that as he watched them. And when she rode Fonteyn to where he stood and dismounted, then flung her arms around his neck and kissed him, Wesley knew he would never ask her to give this up.

"Thank you." Ashton stared into Wesley's eyes and sighed with happiness. "I didn't realise how much I'd missed her, but Fonteyn seems to have forgiven me for leaving her behind."

"I'll bet she'd forgive you most anything," Wesley told her, stroking his fingers down her cheek and drawing one across her bottom lip. "After all, you bring her apples."

Laughing, Ashton took up Fonteyn's reins and led the mare back to the stable block. For the next half hour Wesley watched as she groomed the mare with gentle care, all the while talking to the horse and stroking her attentively.

"There now," Ashton crooned as she locked the bottom half of the stable door and the mare stuck her head out over it. "I'll come and see you later."

Then she turned to Wesley and said, "Just one more

stop to make, I need to see Vanquish."

Ashton had told him about the temperamental horse she was riding in preparation for a higher level of competition. From what she'd told him, Wesley wasn't sure that it was a good thing – but what did he know?

"Hello boy." Ashton reached up to stroke his velvety nose and jumped back when the horse tried to nip her. "Hey, that wasn't very nice," she frowned up at the horse with her hands balled on her hips. "I think you and me need to have ourselves a talk. Do you mind...?" she asked Wesley.

He raised a brow and asked, "Mind what - do you want me to leave you two alone to talk in private?"

"You idiot!" Ashton laughed and batted at his arm. "We talk best when I'm riding him – it won't take long...promise."

This time when he watched her ride, Ashton was firm and demanding, pitting her will against the highly strung horse's and he wasn't sure who was winning.

She hadn't tried taking a jump yet, instead taking the horse on repeated circuits of the paddock. When Wesley caught 'that look' on her face his stomach clenched and his nerves began to buzz.

It was her determined face, the expression she had when the devil took her and Ashton went with it. She turned Vanquish to face a run of fences that would have been challenging even had she been riding Fonteyn. But on Vanquish, who was still occasionally kicking up his back heels, it was foolhardy to Wesley's mind.

Staying absolutely still so as not to distract either horse or rider, he watched with his heart in his mouth.

They cleared the first jump, and then the second easily, but the third jump was a wide spread and higher than the first two. They took off at speed, the horse doing a little dance with its feet to adjust for take-off, and then they were landing safely on the other side. Only then did Wesley realise he had been holding his breath and let it out on a long sigh of relief.

"Bloody hell, he's fierce," Wesley told her when Ashton rode Vanquish to where he stood at the side of the field. "But you seem to have the measure of him."

Dismounting, Ashton gave the horse a pat on his neck while whispering soft encouraging words.

"He's got hell-fire in his veins, but he's a good horse - brave and true once he learns to trust you," she told Wesley with a grin.

They took the horse back to his stall and Ashton gave him a rub down. "I'm not sure you deserve this," she told Vanquish as she held an apple under his nose, her palm flat and inviting him to take it. "No more nipping or there won't be any more."

Wesley waited by the car when Ashton took her things up to her room and got changed. They were going to spend the rest of the afternoon and evening together and he was looking forward it.

Taking a quick shower and pulling on one of her few dresses, Ashton made her way down to where Wesley was waiting for her and felt her heart skip a dozen beats.

He always made her feel like this – shy and excited all at once. She'd taken her hair out of its braid and left it loose because she knew he liked it that way.

His face lit up when he saw her, watched as she walked towards him with studied grace. "You look lovely," Wesley smiled and opened the car door for her.

Glad that she had taken the time to fuss a little, Ashton watched him stride around the car to the driver's side and climb in beside her.

She might be a virgin but she knew sex on legs when she saw it, and Wesley was all that and more, Ashton decided. If only he wouldn't treat me like some sacred virgin that he doesn't want to spoil. I'm a woman and I want my man to want me in bed as well as out of it!

Ashton noticed other women looking at her man when they walked through the car park of a nearby village pub, and they didn't bother to hide their appreciation.

Not entirely confident in their relationship, Ashton

was glad when Wesley put his arm round her waist and pulled her into his side.

She glowed inside. *See, he's mine…look and weep!*

They had a nice pub lunch in the small restaurant and chatted happily for a couple of hours. It seemed they never lacked for conversation and just delighted in each other's company.

"Why are you so worried about Fallon…" Ashton asked as Wesley carried their drinks through to the main pub lounge, "…she won't be stupid enough to go off on her own again – not after the hullaballoo she caused the last time."

"No, well, I bloody hope not," Wesley frowned as they took seats at a window table that looked out over beautiful countryside. "I swear, I'll be the one doing the murdering if she does!"

Chuckling softly, Ashton put a hand over Wesley's and said, "At least you've got me out of your hair for a while. You've got enough to worry about."

He turned to her in amazement. "Is that what you think…that I don't worry about you when you're not with me?"

"I don't know – I suppose I just imagined you too busy on the farm and looking after your family to give me much thought," Ashton told him honestly.

Shaking his head in wonder, Wesley turned his hand up to hold the one she still had laying over it. "You're one of the smartest females I know and yet you're dumb enough to think I don't worry about you?" Closing his eyes for a moment, Wesley let out a long breath and sighed.

"I worry about you every minute of every day. I worry about you eating right and are you getting enough sleep. Then I worry about you getting over-tired, riding one of those horses and breaking your beautiful neck. But most of all, I worry that you'll meet someone – someone who lives the life that you love, a showjumping wizard who might sweep you off your feet leaving me far behind in a memory that will fade all too quickly."

She was flabbergasted, completely flummoxed, and it showed on her lovely face. "You never say anything. You don't seem to mind when you visit then have to leave – I'm always miserable for a day or two after. Tony says I'm like a lovesick puppy."

Again, Wesley can't believe that she doesn't know how it rips him up to leave her at the academy, to go home without her and know he won't see her again for a week or two. But maybe that's my fault? I've been so careful not to tell her that I love her, to give her some room to grow and make her own decisions, maybe I really haven't shown her how very much I care?

"I try not to show you how badly I feel when we have to part," Wesley told her, his thumb gently rubbing over the back of her hand. "But I don't want you to think I don't care – you couldn't be more wrong."

They sat for a while, just looking into each other's eyes and taking in the wonder of the moment. Then Wesley took a leap of faith and declared, "I love you, Ashton. I love your intrepid and fiercely competitive spirit, your sense of loyalty to those you care about, and even your hellish temper tantrums," and he smiled when she rolled her eyes. Then the smile faded and his eyes held hers as he drove the point home, "I love every single bit of who you are – you're my heart, my first thought as day dawns and my last thought when night falls, with a million thoughts of you in between."

CHAPTER THIRTEEN

It was hell trying to concentrate on her routine at the academy. Ashton had thought it would be easier now that she knew how Wesley felt, that he loved her as much as she loved him. But it had become more difficult as the days had gone on, that first thrill of happiness fading into misery the longer they were apart.

Why does it have to be like this – I've known how I felt about him for months now, why is it so much harder now that I know he loves me too?

Her stomach hurt, her appetite had fallen off and her enthusiasm for showjumping was faltering.

She still loved the actual competing – that was something Wesley had been absolutely right about. Her competitive spirit was always on full throttle once she was at the meet and the atmosphere got into her blood.

But the days in between were difficult, gave her time to think about Wesley and how much she wanted to be in his arms. He loved her, that was a miracle that she still hadn't gotten over, and their last parting had been the most painful yet.

Was that because I knew that I was hurting him by being selfish enough to continue living at the academy? It wasn't a consideration before – I always assumed that he went on with his life and never gave me another thought once he'd left. But he does. Wesley loves me – I don't know how I can be this lucky, but he really does love me.

Arriving at the competition ground on the Isle of White, Ashton and Tony busied themselves with preparations for the competition. This would be the first time Ashton competed on Vanquish, a temperamental horse that she was still getting used to.

"Hey, Ashton, how's it going?" Josh asked as he came striding over to the horsebox where Ashton was giving Vanquish some fresh water. "And where is Fonteyn, did you trade her in?"

He was joking, Ashton knew that, but it still made her feel guilty for leaving her own horse behind – like she was betraying Fonteyn by competing on Vanquish.

"You know I'd never do that," Ashton remonstrated, though she managed a small smile. "Tony thinks I need to broaden my riding experience — get ready for the competitions where riders are expected to swap horses and still be able to get clear rounds."

"Hmm, he's right, of course," Josh nodded. "Is this your first time out on him," he asked, reaching out to stroke the arrogant horse's neck.

Vanquish threw up his head and Josh quickly removed his hand and laughed. "Prickly beggar, isn't he?"

"He certainly can be," Ashton confirmed, frowning at Vanquish and studying the horse for a moment. "He's also brave, spirited and as competitive as I am."

"You two should make a good pairing then," Josh chuckled. "Still, watch yourself — don't go all out on him until you're sure it's safe to do so. You could come a cropper if you push before he's ready."

"Are you trying to put me off giving you a run for first place?" Ashton asked with a raised brow.

Hand on his heart, Josh looked affronted. "Would I do that?! I'm only looking out for you — it's not as if this is a life or death competition — it's just a practice really."

"You keep telling yourself that..." she grinned, "...and I'll remind you, you said it when I take first place!"

Still, Ashton thought about Josh's advice when she walked the course with Tony a little while later. Her trainer was full of handy tips and snippets of advice to help her get the best out of the course, and out of Vanquish too.

"Just take it easy – this is a try-out for you and Vanquish to get to know and trust each other a little more. There's plenty of other competitions in the pipeline – just see this one as an extended training session," Tony advised.

She was sitting atop Vanquish, walking him towards the competition ring when she heard someone call her name.

"Ashton – hey, Ashton."

And then she saw him - struggling through the crowd desperately trying to reach her was Wesley.

She grinned down at him as he finally came to stand beside Vanquish. "Hell, I didn't think I was going to make it – good luck and be careful," he warned with a grin.

"I thought you said you couldn't make this one," Ashton told him, returning Wesley's grin, her heart bursting with love at the sight of him.

"Didn't think I could – Matt's helping out while I'm here – one of the benefits of telling everyone about us," he told her as they walked along.

Listening to the commentary at the end of the current rider's round, they heard the result given and the next contender announced.

"We're up – see you after," she told Wesley, and rode into the competition ring as the previous rider exited.

"Ok boy, just take it easy and enjoy the trip out," she told the horse while giving the side of his neck a pat.

Steering him towards the starting point, Ashton listened to the announcer giving a few brief details of her previous wins and then they were ready.

It was a bit unnerving when Vanquish decided to kick up his back legs just before the start, but Ashton managed to take him over the first couple of easy jumps to settle him down.

The third was more difficult, a high spread that lead into a double and then a left turn to take the water jump. Vanquish was still kicking up his back legs at odd moments and Ashton was having to use all her skill and concentration to complete the round.

When they took the last fence to get a clear round the crowd gave her a big round of applause and the announcer congratulated her on a difficult ride.

"That was a good round," Tony told her as Ashton dismounted Vanquish back at the horsebox. "You did exactly right – gave him his head when he needed it but kept him under control between the jumps. You'll both learn a lot from this," he continued as he took the reins from Ashton and tied them to the back of the open horsebox doors.

"He did well – I didn't feel like he was trying to unseat me," Ashton replied when Tony turned back to her. "Just a bit of high spirits – we're both ready to go up against the clock."

But Tony was already shaking his head. "I don't want you to push it too hard – he's not like Fonteyn. Just give him another chance to get used to you and you to him – there'll be other competitions where you'll be able to get more out of him," Tony advised sagely.

"You're the boss," Ashton agreed, and looked around the crowds for Wesley.

She was disappointed when he didn't come back to see her and went in for the second round hoping to spot him before starting.

Damn! Still, it is a big crowd – probably didn't want to lose his place. I'll see him soon enough, afterwards.

Vanquish seemed a little more settled but eager for the off and Ashton decided not to hold back completely.

They were doing well, were on target to beat the last rider at least and maybe even to take the lead. His movements were more fluid this time, Vanquish seeming to be in the moment with Ashton and moving confidently.

Taking a right turn, Ashton and Vanquish took the last but one fence and had a pole down, then sailed over the last fence to applause for a good effort from the crowd.

She was disappointed, but happy with the way her horse had performed.

"Ok, that was better," Tony smiled, no sign of disappointment on his face, Ashton noted. "You pushed it just right, challenged him without taking too much risk. With more training time on him, you and Vanquish should be ready to go for it the next time you compete."

Ashton was relieved to see Wesley when he came to see her just moments after she'd unsaddled Vanquish.

"Hey, that was a terrific ride – I was nervous after the first round antics, but you handled him well," Wesley told her, looking to Tony for confirmation.

"Absolutely! You two are going to do well together," Tony decreed, then slipped away to give the young couple some time together.

"I can't help feeling a bit disappointed," Ashton fessed up with a rueful smile. "A clear round would have been better, even if we didn't make the jump-off."

Wesley was just glad that she was safe.

"You did enough for a first time out with a new horse," he told her, putting his arms around Ashton and breathing her in. He was a farmer, the smell of horses and everything that goes with them were nothing new to him – they didn't even register as he buried his nose in her hair.

When her arms came around him, Wesley felt whole again and Ashton snuggled into his broad chest.

"I've missed you so much," she told him. "I thought it would get better as the days went by after you left, but it just seems to get worse."

He didn't like the thought of her pining for him, yet Wesley felt ten feet tall with pride and happiness.

"It's not forever," he reassured her. "Once you've established yourself and Tony is happy for you to continue training on your own, you can base yourself at home and maybe go to the academy for a week or so each month."

Raising her head to look at him, Ashton's eyes glowed with hope and love. "You really think? I'll talk to Tony tonight, see if it's something the academy would consider."

Then his lips were on hers, soft yet eager, all the kisses he'd dreamed of giving her pouring into this one perfect moment.

They were both breathless when they broke apart, and Ashton looked around them becoming aware of where they were. "I'll get Vanquish rubbed down, fed and watered, then I'll ask Tony if we can look around the show for a while."

Working together, the jobs didn't take long to complete and Tony was more than happy to give them a couple of hours before he and Ashton had to head back to the academy.

Walking with arms around each other's waists, they looked at the many stalls and made their way to the small fairground.

They queued up for the big wheel and snuggled up to each other as it moved to let other passengers on.

"At least you not getting to the jump-off gave us more time together," Wesley smiled, then dipped his head to place a quick kiss on her upturned and smiling lips.

"I knew there was an up-side," she grinned, then turned to take in the expansive view as the big wheel began to turn again.

"Beautiful," Wesley breathed, but he didn't have eyes for anyone or anything other than Ashton.

When she looked at him, Ashton felt her stomach flip over and it had nothing to do with the ride they were on.

"I'll talk to Tony, there has to be a way around this," she told him. "I can't bear all these interminable separations – they're killing me."

CHAPTER FOURTEEN

Back at the academy, Ashton was nervous, pacing her room and trying to work out her argument for living at home while continuing to train part-time at the academy.

It's not like she wouldn't be committed to all the competitions Tony might want her to enter – Matt had always gotten her to them before hadn't he. And if Tony wanted her to go down to the academy the day before a competition, she'd be up for that too.

But what about Vanquish – she was just gaining his trust and she knew Tony wanted her to work with him a lot more.

Well if she was supposed to be preparing for the competitions where you had to swap horses then this would be more realistic. You didn't get to practice on the other riders horses in such competitions, you just had to go out there and take control.

Yes, that was a good argument – Tony could hardly refute that point.

But Vanquish was supposed to be her backup ride - getting to know him as well as she did Fonteyn was supposed to be in preparation for selection to the Olympic team where she would need more than one horse even to be considered.

Well hell! Ashton flopped down on the bed and stared up at the ceiling. There just had to be a way around it. There just had to be, and that was that!

Feeling restless and fidgety, Ashton took herself off to the stables and had a conversation with Fonteyn while she brushed her coat, just a soothing rhythm meant to pamper rather than properly groom.

"I don't see why it couldn't work – I'd make sure you came home with me then bring you back in our horsebox whenever Tony needed me too," Ashton explained to the mare. "I mean, it's not like you aren't used to travelling – we used to go all over the place with Matt and we still travel loads with Tony – so what's the difference?"

But Ashton didn't feel like she was winning this one-sided argument. Her conscience was bothering her, the academy had been good to her and now she was looking to short change them – or that's how it felt.

"We've got jumps at home…" Ashton began again, now tackling Fonteyn's long mane, "…Pam got them in for the riding lessons and is building them up to put on gymkhanas. We managed well enough before all this, didn't we," she asked Fonteyn who was busily pulling hay from the net hung on the wall of her stall.

Putting the brush away, Ashton sat on a clean patch of straw with her back against the wall. She was miserable, missing Wesley so bad that her chest felt like it had a whole in it, and she wrapped her arms around herself for comfort.

The following day she trained with Tony, this time riding Fonteyn, but still she couldn't pull herself out of the doldrums.

She did everything Tony asked of her as he asked it, but Ashton couldn't have told you what she'd been doing even 5 minutes before. It was all going in one ear and out the other, and Tony finally called a halt.

"Ok, stop, we need to talk," Tony told her, standing with hands on his hips and regarding Ashton with concern.

When she dismounted and walked Fonteyn to where he stood, Ashton was genuinely confused. She hadn't done anything wrong, that she could remember. She'd carried out his instructions to the letter, hadn't she?

Truth be told, Ashton wasn't sure, but she thought she had.

"What's going on?" Tony demanded brusquely. "If you no longer want to be here just have the guts to say so – don't waste my time just going through the motions. It isn't good enough – you're not good enough," he told her, shocking Ashton into looking at him, her eyes more alert.

"What do you mean – I've done everything you asked – I didn't do anything wrong," she stated angrily. And, to her surprise, Tony actually looked pleased to see it.

"Well, at least you're still in there," he told her, tapping her head with the knuckles of his left hand. "I was beginning to wonder if the body snatchers had replaced you with a dummy," he told her, referring to an old film that was more his era than hers.

"What...?" she frowned up at him.

"Never mind – before your time," he grimaced. "Just tell me what's eating at you – you're losing weight and you didn't have that much on you in the first place. Is this something to do with Wesley – does he want you to give up and go home?"

Fonteyn began pulling on her reins and Ashton let them fall so that the mare could wander off and graze.

"It isn't that, Wesley is all for me taking this opportunity and making the most of it," Ashton began to explain, but she couldn't keep the misery out of her eyes.

"But you've had enough…?"

"No. No. Really, I still love showjumping." Then she hesitated but held Tony's gaze. "It's just…I really miss home – and yes, I really miss Wesley. But I do still want to train…I just don't know if what I want is possible."

"Tell me what that is and I'll let you know if we can work around it," Tony told her.

Taking a deep breath, Ashton plunged in with an explanation of what she and Wes had come up with then just waited for Tony to knock her back.

"Hmm, you've obviously given this some thought," he mused, rubbing a hand over his chin. "But for it to work, you'd have to be even more dedicated than you are now. You won't have me driving you on, you'd be responsible for the hours you put in and you would have to commit at least one week in four to living at the academy," Tony stipulated.

He still hadn't said it was possible, that the academy would accept her plan, but Ashton was more hopeful now that Tony was giving it serious thought.

"I'll put it to Ms Wentworth and see what she says." Then he smiled, chucked her under the chin and told her to cheer up or she'd frighten the horses. "I might even be persuaded to give your plan my backing…" Tony smiled and shook his head, knowing himself for a soft-hearted fool, "…if you get back on that horse and show me what you're made of."

She did so happily, almost skipping to Fonteyn and swinging herself up into the saddle in a very athletic move.

Tony was impressed, though he tried to hide his grin. She was his favourite student by a mile, and if he could get Clara Wentworth to agree to the compromise, he would take her right to the top of the showjumping world.

The week had dragged — once Tony had told her that she had the go-ahead to implement her plan, Ashton had wanted to do so right away.

But Wesley hadn't been able to get away from the farm until the weekend, and now she stood at the front of the big house waiting for him to arrive.

When Matt's horse box drove up the drive, Ashton began bouncing up and down on the spot, her suitcase at her side. He was here. Wesley was driving and he'd come to fetch her and Fonteyn, to take them home for two wonderful weeks before she would have to return.

But then she would only be at the academy for a week and he'd come to fetch her home again — she could live with that.

When he climbed out of the cab, his long lean legs

clad in jeans and his expansive chest impressively covered by a fitted white t-shirt, Ashton all but swooned at the sight of him.

He laughed when she flung her arms about his neck, hugging him so tightly that she very nearly cut off his airway. But he picked her up and swung her around, as happy as she that he was here to take her home.

Sliding her down his body to her feet, Wesley took possession of her mouth then hummed with delight. "You taste even better than you look, and you look heavenly."

She blushed, but Ashton was thrilled that he looked ready to devour her at any moment.

"Come on, we have to get Fonteyn and then we can go," Ashton reminded him.

The mare was calm and didn't need much persuasion to enter the back of the horsebox. Ashton made sure that Fonteyn had a net of fresh hay in the back with her and plenty of soft bedding on the floor.

Wesley had stowed her suitcase in the cab at the back of the seats, and once Ashton had climbed in and put her seatbelt on, they were off.

When they turned out of the gates and onto the main road, Wesley turned a sideways look at Ashton and couldn't restrain his grin.

She let out an excited scream and stomped her feet

on the floor of the cab in a rapid happy dance, her fists pumping the air to match the beat of her feet.

"Do I take it you're happy to be going home?" he chuckled, his eyes bright with his own glee.

"You most certainly do," Ashton agreed, her smile so wide it was making her cheeks ache. "Oh Wes, just to be able to see each other every day will be heaven – I can't tell you how miserable I've been since you left."

He looked at her more closely when they pulled up for a red light, and took in her loss of weight. "You need feeding up – my mother will soon take care of that."

Resting her head back on the seat, Ashton took in a deep breath then let it out slowly, allowing her brain to accept the simple truth. She was going home, would eat meals with Wesley's family if she wanted to, could go out for a walk with him whenever they chose and the time they spent apart would be minimal in comparison to previous months.

Life just didn't get much better than that.

Everyone was there when the horsebox pulled up outside the main house on Langdon Farm. Matt hugged his sister and took the suitcase Wesley handed down from the cab, Chad frowned and told Ashton that she needed to look after herself more, then Pam and Lizzy both trudged up from the stables to hug her and welcome her home.

Jackson and Mac held back while the family fussed then made their way to the back of the horsebox to get Fonteyn.

The mare was happy enough to be let out, flaring her nostrils in the fresh air.

"Thanks, Jackson," Ashton told the tall man who was leading her horse to the stables. Then she flung her arms around his father's neck and said, "I'm so glad to be home, Mac – did you miss me?"

Embarrassed by her open show of affection, Mac patted her back then drew away. "It's been quiet without you around," he smiled. "No doubt the place will liven up some now that you're home."

She laughed happily, nodding in agreement. "I like to think I make my mark on the place," Ashton chuckled.

"Be in no doubt of that," Mac told her. "No doubt at all."

Matt told her to go in with Wesley and he'd take the horsebox down to the stables to park it in its usual spot. He took the time to clean it out, then made his way back up to the house. The family was back together and there would be a special meal to celebrate tonight.

Shooing the girls out of the kitchen, Matt cooked one of his specialties and served up chilli-con-carne for everyone.

"Jesus, Matt, this is lovely," Ashton congratulated him. "You'll have to teach me how to make it so that I can make it for Wesley when we're married."

The chatter at the table stopped and Chad looked from Ashton to Wesley.

Wesley was coughing on the mouthful of food that he'd just swallowed the wrong way and couldn't get a word out. But Ashton just lifted her chin and sent her brother a defiant look.

"Which won't happen for a while yet, and not at all if Wesley doesn't hurry up and ask me," she stated, turning a smile to her recovering boyfriend.

He shook his head at her and had to remind himself that this is what he loved about Ashton – she didn't mince her words and certainly wasn't backwards at coming forwards, and he'd just have to deal with it.

"If I live through this meal I might just consider doing so," Wesley chuckled after taking a restorative sip of wine. "In the meantime, eat," he ordered. "You've lost far too much weight and I don't like my women skinny!"

It was Ashton's turn to splutter and cough, turning to look at Wesley with barely restrained outrage.

"You get what you get," she told him.

But Wesley shook his head, enjoying himself now he'd recovered from the shock. "Not if you expect me to marry you – a bag of bones won't keep me warm on a chilly night."

Before Ashton could think of a rejoinder, Pam had risen from her seat and asked her to help dish up the pudding Matt had prepared.

With ill grace, Ashton followed her future sister-in-law out to the kitchen and shot Wesley a look that might have withered a lesser man.

"He is so full of himself," Ashton told Pam. "As if I'd try to make myself into the woman of his dreams – well he can dream on if he expects that!"

"Isn't that what we all do?" Pam asked quietly, scooping portions of apple crumble into dishes. "I know I try to be what Matt needs, what would be the point of doing otherwise?"

She had to think about that, and did so while she poured homemade custard over the crumble.

She knew she'd lost weight recently, and it's not like she'd done so deliberately. For christ's sake, it was his fault – or at least, it was all about him. She'd been pining for him, had been unable to eat half the time, the hole in her chest just too big and too painful to ignore.

Ashton sulked for another minute then gave herself a mental shake down to cast off the silly annoyance she felt. This was too good a day to let a stupid comment spoil it.

And when it came right down to it, she did want to please him, wanted Wesley to find her attractive and knew it wasn't just her body he was after.

Hell, apart from some heavy petting he hadn't even tried to get her clothes off. Annoying really.

<u>CHAPTER FIFTEEN</u>

It was heaven, Ashton was living the dream – she worked hard at her training, travelled to the academy and the competitions that Tony entered her for, and she saw Wesley almost every day.

The week she had committed to living at the academy once a month, passed quickly and was really quite enjoyable.

Ok, she missed Wesley but they talked every evening on the phone and he caught her up with everything at home – like the news that her parents were due back at the weekend.

"Matt said they sounded really excited about the house he's found them," Wesley told her. "He still hasn't let on that he had it built for them – he showed me around it yesterday and I have to say, it's great. The garden is looking like it's always been there, sort of homey and welcoming."

"I can't believe it's been a whole year since they left," Ashton sighed. "I wasn't too happy with the idea when my dad first suggested it, but mum certainly deserved to see a bit of the world – she put everything on hold to take care of us lot."

"And that included me and Fallon for a lot of the time," Wesley observed, remembering all the times he and his sister had spent at the Langdon's. "I want that childhood for our kids," Wesley told her softly.

Her heart lurched at the vision he'd put in her head, and Ashton felt her eyes tear up. "A bit presumptuous aren't you – you still haven't asked me to marry you."

She heard his low chuckle and couldn't resist the smile that tugged at her lips.

"I'm getting around to it…maybe – have you started putting any of that weight you lost back on yet?"

She knew he was just looking out for her, but it still annoyed Ashton. "If I have it's because my appetite is back – I don't eat just because you tell me to!"

Now the laughter she heard was full and happy. "We are going to have one hell of a life together," Wes told her, the laughter still in his voice. "I wonder what your parents will make of us when they get home – telling them about us on the phone is one thing, seeing us together might be quite another."

Considering that, Ashton frowned and asked, "Are you nervous? Do you think they'll disapprove?"

Taking a moment to mull that over, Wesley replied, "You're 18 and I'm almost 25, they might consider me too old for you."

"Well that's just stupid!" Ashton declared hotly, but the idea of her parent's disapproval did make her stomach lurch. "I'm old enough to make up my own mind and so are you – are you telling me that you won't marry me if my parents don't give us their blessing?"

He didn't answer right away, but took the time to get his thoughts straight. "I love you, you already know that, but if your parents were dead set against us, I'm not sure I'd want the kind of marriage that would estrange you from your family. It wouldn't be right."

"That's why you haven't proposed," she said dully, the realisation stabbing right through her. "And you won't, not if my parents aren't all for it."

"No," he admitted. "It just wouldn't be right."

That night had been hellish to get through, even her dreams were filled with images of Wes walking away from her and her sobbing, her heart broken into tiny pieces.

Looking in the bathroom mirror, Ashton saw a ghost

looking back at her. Her usually bright eyes were sunken into her head, her cheeks were pale and everything about her expression said 'shattered'.

And she was. How could Wesley say such things – if they were in love then didn't that mean they would battle whatever came at them together? That's what love and marriage was all about…wasn't it?

She had to force down some breakfast, the noise of the dining room with its happy chatter passing her by unnoticed.

It was painful even to contemplate a future without Wesley in it – and worse, a future where she would have to see him marry someone else.

It was clear that he was ready to settle down, wanted a wife and children to live with him on the Craemer farm. But that was her future, wasn't it? Her parents weren't so small minded as to stand in the way of her happiness just because Wesley was a few years older than her, were they?

Six years, that's all they were talking about – her own dad was four years older than her mother, surely they wouldn't quibble about another 2.

She sat pushing food around her plate for another few minutes then Ashton decided to take a walk down to the stables.

There was more than one training paddock set up with jumps and already in use. She watched a girl she was friendly with going through a routine with her coach then continued walking to Fonteyn's stall.

The mare greeted her with a whinny and a snort, stomping her feet impatiently.

"Hey, I'm not that late," Ashton told the mare as she undid the stable door and locked it behind her. She took the time to pet Fonteyn, to talk to her and enjoy the company of her best friend. "You never criticise or chastise me..." Ashton crooned softly, "...and more importantly, you never judge me wanting. I love him, Fonteyn – Wesley is the future I've been dreaming of, the only future I want."

The mare rubbed her head against Ashton's shoulder in what felt like a show of support.

"You see, even you know it's the right thing – loving someone who is a few years older isn't such a big deal." But Ashton worried that it might be, that her parent's might find it too big a deal to accept.

Gathering up Fonteyn's water bucket and empty hay net, Ashton went off to fill them with fresh. Then she got out the mucking out kit and set to work raking out the soiled straw and cleaning the stall.

By the time she'd done everything to her satisfaction,

Ashton was feeling a little better. She'd decided not to be so pessimistic. Her parents were good and loving people, she had to trust that they would put her happiness above all else. They always had before, hadn't they?

But she heard that little voice in her head say 'yes, when it's been in your best interest.'

She was sat on the steps of the large academy house when Wesley came to take her home the next day, and he could see the sadness in her posture.

It tore at him that he was responsible for making her feel that way, but he'd had to be honest and open about the situation as he saw it.

He'd struggled with it, had turned the situation over in his mind until his head had felt like exploding. But he hadn't been able to see a future for them without her parent's approval.

What kind of life would that be for Ashton – to know that her family lived on the neighbouring farm but didn't want to know her? Her father was a strong character, if he decided to cut her off it would be swift and final, of that Wesley was sure. And Ashton marrying someone he didn't approve of would be a good enough reason for him to do so – he just couldn't let that happen.

If he truly loved Ashton, and he did, then he would have to love her enough to walk away

But for now, for this last day until her parent's got home, they were free to love and be with each other and he intended to make the most of it.

"Come on, princess – you look like you got tossed out of the castle with that sad face and your suitcase at your side," Wesley grinned as he walked towards Ashton.

But she didn't laugh as he'd wanted her to. Instead Ashton sprang to her feet and flung her arms around his neck, burying her face into him and breathing in the scent of her man.

When his arms came around her, Ashton felt the muscles in his arms, hard and strong they made her feel safe. His heart beat next to her heart, his warmth mingled with her own – they may not have made love yet, but they were one in every way that mattered. No one would take him away from her. No one.

"Hey. Hey," he crooned in her ear, gently smoothing a hand down her beautiful red hair. "We're ok. We're fine. Let's enjoy today and leave tomorrow to take care of itself."

For a moment she hugged him closer, then Ashton took a step back and smiled up at him. "I think that's a fine idea, let's start that process now."

Stepping back into his arms, Ashton pulled his head down and took his lips in a sizzling kiss that all but blew the top of his head off. If she had been trying to prove a point, then it was one well made – Wesley was drowning in her, losing all coherent thought and sense of where they were.

When she stepped back again, her grin was wicked. "Just a taste of what you'll be living without if you dare to leave me," Ashton smiled sexily. "And we haven't even gotten to the good part yet."

Oh she'd stirred him up alright. Wesley was looking at her through eyes dark with wanting and it took all his self-control not to pull her back into his arms for another taste. But that would have been masochistic at best, he told himself while forcing one foot in front of the other to go back to the car.

"I should paddle your backside for that," he told her, and had to shift in his seat to make his now too tight jeans more comfortable.

But Ashton wasn't concerned, she just smiled and cocked a brow at him. "Is that some kind of foreplay – I've read about how some men like the kink."

His mouth dropped open, then Wesley let out a howling laugh and shook his head in wonder. "I never know what is going to come out of your mouth next. You are one of a kind, that's a fact."

Happy with that assessment, Ashton merely shrugged. "Good, then you'll never get bored with me."

Still smiling, Wesley again shook his head, "I don't think that would be possible."

<u>CHAPTER SIXTEEN</u>

They'd had a wonderful afternoon and evening together, but as Ashton woke and sat up in bed her first thoughts were filled with worry.

Until Wes had voiced his concerns over her parent's acceptance of them as a couple, Ashton hadn't given it a thought. Matt had told them about her and Wes as soon as he himself had been told – but he'd never relayed any concerns her parent's might have had, and he would have, she was certain of that.

But did that mean they didn't have them – or were they just waiting until they got home to voice those concerns face to face with her and Wes.

Scrubbing at her scalp with her short fingernails, Ashton pinned up her long hair and headed for the shower.

She couldn't worry about this for hours on end, it just wasn't like her. She would deal with whatever happened, would fight her corner if her parents really did raise objections. But at the end of the day none of it mattered.

Stepping into the shower, Ashton was quick and efficient, stepping out of it again less than five minutes later. She toweled off briskly, took care of her other needs then headed back to the bedroom to get dressed.

She'd heard some movement in the house earlier, probably Matt, Pam and Lizzy getting up to begin their work on the farm and stables. But she'd drifted off to sleep again and now had no idea of the time.

Stepping into jeans, Ashton rummaged in her wardrobe for a top to go with them. She pulled out a lightweight short-sleeved jumper in deepest plum and held it up in front of her to judge the effect in the long dress mirror.

Not usually vain, Ashton shook her head at her reflection and chuckled with wry derision. "He won't even notice – men are notoriously blind when it comes to women doing their hair or dressing carefully for them," she whispered, and again shook her head at her own silliness.

Fallon had told her loads about Chad and Ashton had been shocked to hear it. Like how she had treated herself to having her hair done at a salon, had bought a lovely new outfit for their evening out and Chad hadn't even blinked.

Men just don't 'see' women. They get an overall picture of you in their head and stick with it - change something and they still see the old you. It's a complete waste of time

Well, Ashton would give Wes the benefit of the doubt until he proved her wrong, and even smeared her lips with a little gloss after brushing her hair to a salon shine.

When, an hour later, Ashton walked into the Craemer's kitchen and Wes told her how lovely she looked, she smiled to herself and gave him top marks for observation.

"Are your parents back yet?" he asked, feigning only mild interest.

But he couldn't fool her, Ashton knew that he was on tenterhooks, deeply worried that her father would call a halt to their seeing each other.

She took a seat at the breakfast table as he moved to make her a cup of tea. "Mum and Fallon are upstairs — housework stuff," he clarified when he turned and handed her a mug.

"If you need to get on I'll just drink this tea and see you later," Ashton offered, noting that Wes was in his work clothes.

"No need. I just have a couple of jobs to do – they won't take me above an hour if you want to hang around," Wes told her.

He was still standing, leaning his tall frame back against the sink and looking into his mug of tea rather than drinking it.

Putting her mug on the table, Ashton rose and went to him, took the mug out of his hand and put it down. Then she just put her arms around his waist and leaned into him.

His arms came around her and Wesley laid his cheek on top of her head. "I'm afraid of losing you. I've waited all this time and now…"

He couldn't finish the thought, just tightened his arms around Ashton and breathed her in.

"You won't lose me," she whispered into his chest, loving the warmth and strength of him. "I have a right to make my own choices…and I chose you," she told him, leaning back just enough to look into his sad eyes.

The breath of a sigh that whispered between them just before he took her lips, made Ashton shiver inside. But she wasn't weak and determined to show Wesley that she was all woman and all his!

She took over the kiss, moved it from gentle and loving to demanding and intimate. Her tongue found his and they slid against each other so blatantly suggestive that it wasn't long before she felt Wesley harden against her.

Drawing back just a fraction of an inch, Ashton looked hot and sexy as she looked him straight in the eye. "If we were alone right now, I'd give you everything because it's mine to give. I'm all grown up, Wes, I don't need you to protect me anymore."

He knew exactly what she meant, could visualise them standing in that cold river. He had barely been able to tear himself away from her, had dived headlong into the cold water in a bid to free himself from the desperate need he'd had for her. But even then, Ashton had returned his feelings, as unsure and naïve as they had been.

Pulling her back into his arms, Wesley held her there for a moment longer then let her go. "We'll know where we stand soon enough. Now finish your tea, I'm going to get those jobs done."

With that he was gone and Ashton was left alone to mull things over. If he thinks he can shake me off if my dad disapproves…well, he'd better think again! I'm 18, will be 19 in another couple of months, so just let anybody try telling me I'm not old enough to make up my own damn mind – I'd rather move out on my own than lose Wesley!

For the next hour Ashton thought about that idea.

True, she didn't earn a fortune from her showjumping, but some of the purses had been heavy enough to bank and were building into a nice little nest-egg.

And she could go pro. There were competitions out there, international competitions that paid huge amounts to the winners. In time she'd have to buy another horse, of course – maybe Matt would let her use the farm's horsebox until she could afford one of her own – he'd only ever used it to ferry her and Fonteyn to competitions anyway.

Her dad might object to Matt helping her out, might see it as aiding and abetting, but it was her decision and she didn't think Matt would stand back and watch her struggle – he had more spine than that.

Chad was another matter – he might side with her dad. He hadn't put any barriers in the way of her seeing Wesley, but she knew he had concerns.

And then it came to her, she had to get Chad on side. Had to get to him and gain his support before the shit hit the fan. Her dad would listen to him, had always listened to Chad, though she had no idea why.

Getting up from the table, Ashton put her empty mug in the sink and went outside. She got on Fonteyn just as Wesley was rounding the house to come back inside, and she waved, shouting over at him.

"I'll see you later – I have a marriage to save!"

Damn it! He'd worked hard to get his jobs done and get back to her, now Ashton was taking off like a bat out of hell. And what the hell was she on about – a marriage to save? Had Pam or Matt called her – were they having a row, threatening to call off the wedding?

Hell if he knew what was going on, but he'd be there for Matt if there really was a problem. It had been like that all their lives – Chad, Matt and Wesley, if one had a problem the other two had waded in to help them solve it. Even if that had meant getting a black eye or just going down the pub to drown their sorrows.

Ashton's dad had tagged them 'The Three Musketeers', and it had been true, they were 'all for one and one for all', whatever it took.

When Ashton got back to the stables, she hailed Lizzy and asked her for a favour. "I really need to speak to Chad – would you mind taking care of Fonteyr for me?"

The young girl could see the urgency in Ashton's eyes and nodded quickly. "No problem, you go."

Then Ashton took off running, ran into the house and straight up to her brother's room where she knew he spent most of his time.

When she threw open the door to his room, Ashton didn't notice that Chad was tapping away at a laptop on his desk by the window, nor did she see the part manuscript he'd printed out and edited, but she did register his annoyance and quickly tried to explain.

"I need your help," Ashton declared dramatically, promptly turning to pace the room. "You're my brother – the eldest – you're responsible for looking after us, you've always said so," she turned to him, an accusatory look in her determined eyes.

Swivelling his chair, Chad met her stare with a calm one of his own. "And you've always told me that I'm not the boss of you, that you can take care of yourself perfectly well." He had to control the smile that wanted to ruin his stiff façade, and waited for his sister to get to the point.

"Well, that's true, mostly," she conceded with a frown, beginning to pace the room again, giving herself time to formulate a strategy. "But what if I needed you – what if my whole future were in your hands – would you stand by me, or would you side with them?"

His dark head tipped to one side a little as Chad regarded her. "Ashton, if this is some silly-"

"It's not!" she jumped in. "I'm perfectly serious. This is one time that I'm asking you for help. Hell, I'll get down on my knees and beg if that's what it takes."

But Chad was already shaking his head and waved

towards the nearby bed. "Sit. Tell me what's going on and I'll give you my answer."

But to his surprise Ashton stayed standing and her face turned mutinous. "No. You've always stood by Matt no matter what, now I'm asking you to do the same for me. It shouldn't matter what it is, only that I need you and that you care enough to help me."

This was a rare moment – Chad had never known Ashton to ask for help, even when she had so obviously needed it. It was one of the things he'd loved about her as they had been growing up.

Despite the fact that he'd berated his sister often, had tried to stop her doing idiotic and dangerous things in a bid to prove herself, Chad had, even then, admired her spirit.

But what could Ashton possibly want so badly that she was willing to come to him – to beg for his help, if that's what he asked of her.

"Alright, if whatever it is means that much to you, I'll stand by you no matter what," Chad told her, and watched her eyes go wide with shock.

When her lips trembled and those wide eyes filled with tears, Chad stood and took her arms. "What is it?"

"I love Wesley, and he thinks dad will disapprove of us, because of the age difference," Ashton finally managed to get the words out. "He said he'd walk away rather than estrange me from my family, but I'll die if I lose him. I know I will."

So, this is what had got his sister so riled up. Ashton was afraid their father would separate her and Wesley and Wesley was too honourable to go against him.

"Don't be so dramatic," Chad told her, steering Ashton to sit in his chair while he sat on the edge of the bed. "You obviously think there's a possibility that Wesley is right, so what do you expect me to do about it?"

"Dad listens to you," she exclaimed, leaning forward in the chair with an earnest expression. "If he thinks we have your approval he won't get on his high horse and lay the law down. You know how dad can be — he's always seen me as his little girl. But I'm not…" she told Chad, straightening her back, visibly toughening up, "…I'm a woman, and I'm entitled to be with the man I love — whatever that takes."

Narrowing his eyes, Chad looked at his little sister and realised that she was right. But that didn't mean he would give in to her every demand.

"And what does that mean?" he asked quietly, his voice dark and dangerous.

Ashton knew that voice, knew the threat behind it. Push Chad too far and he would come down hard on you, and that was the last thing she wanted.

"Only that if you won't help me, I'll have to find another way. I love Wesley, and I won't let him walk away from me out of some misplaced chivalry."

<u>CHAPTER SEVENTEEN</u>

When a taxi drew up outside the Langdon house it didn't take long for a crowd to form around it.

Avis and Charles Langdon had been travelling for a year, making up for all the holidays they never took and to celebrate their retirement from the farm.

Excited hugs were exchanged, then Chad and Matt helped the taxi driver to unload all the luggage.

"Christ, how did they get all this from one place to another," Matt asked, tilting an overlarge suitcase onto its wheels and dragging it into the house.

Chad followed with a second, slightly smaller suitcase and a matching holdall. It took several trips to ferry everything inside as there were numerous carrier bags filled with gifts and souvenirs.

Mac shook hands with Charley, told him it was nice to

have him back and introduced him to his son, Jackson.

"How do you do, Mr Langdon," Jackson held out a hand to his father's old boss.

When Charley took it, Jackson was impressed by the older man's firm grip and the acutely assessing eyes that weighed him up.

"I've been hearing good things about you," Charley told him. "Matt's been keeping me up to date with things, says you're as handy around the farm as Mac here."

Jackson smiled and said, "Praise indeed. We all work well together and the jobs get done in a timely manner. You have a very large, very well run farm here."

"Not mine now," Charley replied, just an edge of a smile tugging at his lips. "We left this to the children, all of them, but it seems to have fallen onto Matt's shoulders in the end."

"He's doing a fine job," Mac chimed in. "Matt and Pam make a good team, just like you and Avis did for so many years. The farm's in good hands, Charley."

At 6ft 5", Charles Langdon stood tall and proud, his weathered face still handsome despite the years that had etched themselves on it.

"That's good to know – always thought it would be Chad who took the reins over, but Matt's a Langdon through and through – he'll do just as well."

Pam and Lizzy had come up from the stables after Ashton had gone to fetch them. "My mother's dying to meet you, Lizzy and she's already been asking after you, Pam."

"Are they really tanned," Pam enquired just before they stepped through the front door.

But Avis forestalled Ashton's answer when she came out of the sitting room and caught Pam up in a warm hug. "Oh Pam – it's such good news about you and our Matt. We always thought it was on the cards, but…"

Avis had to break off as she reached into her pocket to get a tissue and dry her eyes.

"I'm going to need some help with the wedding plans…" Pam told Matt's tearful mother, "…my mother's arthritis is only getting worse – she wouldn't manage the shops or the stress."

Beaming with happiness, Avis immediately agreed. "What a wonderful gift that will be. But I hope your dad is well enough to walk you down the aisle."

Pam's parents had had her late in life and, now in their middle sixties, they were both suffering from chronic infirmities.

"We've talked to them about the arrangements – mum's happy for us to arrange everything and dad said nothing would stop him from giving his daughter away,"

Pam smiled, a few tears gathering in her own eyes.

"Women! Mention weddings and the waterworks start," Charley declared as the two women entered the sitting room. "It's supposed to be a happy occasion but you'd never know it with all the crying that goes on."

His eyes narrowed when he spotted Lizzy trying to slip into the room unnoticed. "You must be Lizzy – don't hide yourself away over there – come and sit down."

Feeling everyone's eyes on her, Lizzy nervously moved to sit on the settee, but looking up at the new Mr Langdon from that position only served to make him appear even bigger and all the more scary.

Pam understood how Lizzy felt and moved to sit next to the girl. "Lizzy and I have prepared a chicken casserole for the evening meal – will you be staying for it, or do you want to see your new home?"

"I must admit, I've been really excited about seeing our new house," Avis admitted. "Matt has been very secretive – he wouldn't give us a clue. But if it really wouldn't put things out, we'd love to stay for dinner."

Turning to Lizzy, Pam gave the young girl an encouraging smile and said, "Shall we go and check on everything?"

Lizzy was up and out of her seat in the blink of an eye, then escaped to the kitchen.

"She's just shy," Pam explained before following Lizzy out.

"Well, there have certainly been a lot of changes around here," Avis smiled at her sons and Ashton. "I think I might have time to sort the presents out before dinner is ready."

"Presents." Ashton grinned like a little girl, she'd always loved surprises.

Her mother passed Ashton a long slim box and watched as the young girl opened it.

Her eyes went wide and Ashton gasped.

"Oh mum, dad, they're wonderful," Ashton declared, looking at the pearl ear-studs and picking up the matching pearl necklace to examine it.

"Well, you're all grown up now," her mother told her as she put a hand to Ashton's cheek. "The young girl we left behind a year ago has blossomed into a lovely young woman."

Charles Langdon gave a grunt of disapproval but, much to Ashton's relief, said nothing.

Her eyes flew to look at Chad, pleading for him to come through for her.

Taking his cue, Chad moved to stand behind his sister's chair and said, "It seems Wes agrees with you, mother – he's totally smitten with our Ashton. And I must say, although I wasn't sure about the match, I think they'll make a real go of it."

"Bit of an age gap," Charley snapped, but not with any real bite.

"Only two years more than you and mum," Matt pointed out. "Two years is nothing really."

Looking at his family in turn, Charley huffed. "So, you're ganging up on me – well, we'll just see. I want a word with Wesley Craemer."

Moving to distract her husband, Avis took out two more presents and handed them to Chad and Matt just as Pam and Lizzy returned from the kitchen.

Opening his first, Matt took out a watch. It had a two tone stainless steel strap and a midnight blue face with silver hands, and it was gorgeous.

"Emporio Armani! This is amazing," Matt told them, looking from his mum to his dad with wide shocked eyes.

"Well, you haven't had your old watch repaired, so we thought we'd buy you something special to replace it," his mother told him. "It's supposed to be very reliable and it looks good too."

Passing it to Pam to take a look, Matt turned with interest to see what Chad had got.

His elder brother frowned when he lifted the lid of the box he'd been given only to find a long, slim, brown leather case inside it.

Taking it out, Chad turned the excellently crafted case in his hand then flipped the top flap open. Inside was a fountain pen – a very special, limited edition, Visconti fountain pen.

Getting a very peculiar feeling in his gut, Chad looked at his parents and simply asked, "Why?"

This time it was his father who took the lead, looking at Chad with a raised brow. "Got something to tell us, son?"

They couldn't know, they'd been out of the country for a whole year. No one new, except his publisher.

"I'm not sure what you mean," Chad prevaricated.

"Oh, really." His father's tone sounded sceptical, as he moved to take something from another carrier bag. "We thought you might want a special pen to sign this for us."

"Shit!" Chad breathed the word like an oath – stared dumbfounded at the book his father held out to him.

"We bought it in Italy and bought the pen a couple of days after," Charles Langdon said, regarding his eldest son with some curiosity. "Why on earth didn't you tell us?"

Matt took the book before Chad could and stared at the cover in shocked amazement. "You're an author?!" When Chad nodded Matt grinned, "So that's where you've been getting your money – I began to wonder if you'd taken to a life of crime – instead you're writing about it."

"The second one is due out in a couple of months – I've only just sent the third one in," Chad told them, uncomfortable with the situation but pleased that his family seemed proud of him.

Avis handed a present to Pam and another to Lizzy. "Just a little something," she smiled.

"Oh." Pam took the blue silk scarf from the flat box and let it drape and slide over the back of her hand. "This is lovely – so soft and smooth. Thank you."

When all eyes turned to Lizzy, her bottom lip trembled, holding the small box she'd been given out to Avis. "You shouldn't have," she said quietly. "I'm not family – you should give it to Pam."

But Avis only smiled and pushed the box back to her. "We bought it for you, Lizzy. I know my children consider you family now."

With damp eyes and her bottom lip sucked in to stop it trembling, Lizzy opened the box and took out a silver locket.

"I've never had anything like it," Lizzy said, in awe of the fine silver chain and the beautifully etched oval hanging from it.

"You can put a photo on either side of it," Avis told her, moving to show the girl how to open it.

"I can put the boys in there…and my mum and dad,"

Lizzy said, her thumb caressing the precious metal with true reverence.

"I'll help you do that," Pam offered, touched by the young girl's reaction to being given a gift.

"Thank you," she told Pam. "Thank you so much," Lizzy said to Avis, then dared to extend her gaze to include Charles Langdon.

"I've got small gifts for Jackson and Mac, of course — but they'll have to wait until tomorrow," Avis smiled, happy with the way it had all turned out.

"If everyone's ready, the dinner is about ready to dish up," Pam suggested.

"Thank the Lord for that..." Charley said, a large hand rubbing his belly, "...I'm starving."

CHAPTER EIGHTEEN

The meal over, Avis and Charley were beginning to flag and hinted that it was time to go.

Matt turned to Chad, "We'll take both cars – that way we can get all the luggage in the boots and ferry everyone in one go."

"Is the new house far?" Avis asked her sons.

Chad just smiled while Matt beamed. "Walking distance – but you have too much luggage for that."

Frowning up at her husband, Avis watched Charley shake his head and lift his shoulders in an 'I have no idea' shrug.

Just minutes later, Chad and Matt pulled their cars up outside of their parent's cottage. Everyone piled out of the cars and watched for Avis and Charley's reactions.

They moved to the driveway together, looked at the

beautiful flowers and shrubs and up to the detailed thatch.

Matt watched as his father frowned. "If I didn't know that Seb was retired, I'd have said this was his handiwork."

"And you'd be right," Matt told his father proudly. "When I told him who it was for, Seb was all for it – said the design was a one off...unique."

Everyone followed the couple up to the front door and Matt passed his father a small bunch of keys.

Charley unlocked the door then surprised everyone when he turned to his wife and scooped her up into his strong arms. "This is our very own home – our first," Charley told Avis. "And I'm going to carry my wife across its threshold."

He did so, and when Charley dipped his head to kiss Avis' smiling lips a round of applause and cheers reminded them that they had an audience.

Lowering Avis to stand, Charley cleared his throat then put his arm around her and began the walk through their new home.

"Pam and Lizzy got everything set up and clean," Matt informed them. "We all chipped in with the decorating and the garden – but you've only got to say if you want something changing and we'll see to it."

But as the couple moved through the cottage it became evident that they loved it.

"I wouldn't change a thing," Avis smiled at her family then up to her husband. "We have everything we could ever want," and Charley nodded in agreement.

"The housing project worried me some…" Charles Langdon admitted, looking to Matt, "…but you've done a fine job – given the village a much needed boost."

"Thanks, dad." Matt looked across the sitting room to Pam and saw the pride she wore so openly, and felt his nerves settle.

The Langdons were all back together and the world was right again. Matt felt a great burden lift from his shoulders, though nothing had really changed.

He was still solely in charge of Langdon Farm, still had to balance the books and make sure his staff got paid – but running the farm now took on the old pleasurable air that had burrowed deep into his heart.

Moving to her mother's side, Ashton slid her hand through her arm and smiled. "Come with me, I want to show you something."

Mother and daughter moved out of the sitting room and went through the dining room to the double patio doors. Ashton unlocked them, and when they both stepped out into the garden a movement sensitive light came on.

"Over here," Ashton indicated, guiding her mother across the lawn to a secluded area of the large garden.

There was a lovely bench, lots of flowering shrubs and a beautiful fishpond with a miniature wishing well to the side.

"Oh my goodness." Avis Langdon felt her eyes tear up and turned to her daughter with gratitude and love. "You remembered – but it was years ago."

As a little girl, Ashton remembered her mother telling her stories at bedtime and one of them had been about a secret garden.

The way her mother had described the fishpond and the wishing well had prompted her to ask, "Did you have a garden like that when you were a little girl?"

And her mother had replied, "No, but I often dreamed of having one just like it. I think it would be nice to sit in the sunshine and watch the fish swimming around."

"Is it close to how you imagined it?" Ashton asked nervously, as this had been her particular part of the project.

"It's better," Avis declared, taking her daughter's hand, both of them moving to take a seat on the bench. "There's even fish in the pond already."

"I'll show you where I stocked the fish food when we go back inside," Ashton told her, then nervously bit her bottom lip.

"Thank you, darling." Avis patted her daughter's hand then asked, "And now, will you tell me what's troubling you?"

Letting out a nervous chuckle, Ashton gave her mother a rueful smile. "I should have known nothing gets past you – but you should enjoy your garden and your first night home. We can talk about other things another day."

Avis merely smiled patiently, giving the hand she had patted a gentle rub.

"Ok…" Ashton began reluctantly, "…but it's awkward. I don't really know why it's bothering me, I mean, Wes finally admitted that he loves me, and I really love him…"

"But…?" Avis murmured softly when her daughter hesitated.

"If he really loves me, how could he say that he'd walk away if dad disapproved?" Her eyes looked pained, the hurt so clear that it broke her mother's heart to see it. "I wouldn't, I couldn't let anyone come between us – but Wes said he'd walk away rather than come between me and my family."

Letting her breath out on a quiet sigh, Avis held her daughter's hand and looked at the fish in their beautiful new home.

"I think Wesley must love you very much," Avis

contradicted, nodding at her own thoughts. "To be willing to sacrifice his own happiness in a bid to ensure yours is a selfless act that would take a lot of courage and a great deal of love."

"But I wouldn't be happy," Ashton declared. "How could I be – I love Wes, I want to spend the rest of my life with him. I just don't understand how he could think of walking away from me – how he could walk away if he loves me half as much as I love him."

They sat together watching the fish go round and round, then Avis finally said, "It's one thing to offer, to believe that you would do the noble thing as Wesley sees it – but it would be quite another to follow through. He may have managed to walk away initially, but I doubt he would have stayed away for long.

Wesley was always the one to admit wrong doing first when the boys were young – he has a natural honesty that runs core deep and that, it seems, has matured to encompass honour and dignity. I think it's lovely that he would put your wellbeing before his own."

Ashton frowned, and eventually said, "Well I think he's stupid, and I'll tell him so when he comes over tomorrow." Then she turned to her mother, concern smoothing out the flash of temper, "Will dad be alright about us? He won't drive Wesley away, will he?"

A conspiratorial smile spread over her mother's lovely face. "I'll see to your father – he'll give Wesley a chance to prove that he's capable of looking after you."

When they stood to go back indoors, Ashton flung her arms about her mother's neck and held her tightly. "I've missed you so much. I'm really glad you're back."

The following day, Avis and Charles Langdon invited the first caller to their cottage into their new home.

"It's lovely to see you, Wesley," Avis greeted him, inviting the tall man into the sitting room. "I don't know if I'm shrinking with age, but you seem even taller than the last time I saw you."

Wesley smiled, taking a seat when it was indicated he should do so. "My mother complains that I give her neck-ache," Wes chuckled, though the moment of humour quickly died when he saw how Charles Langdon was looking at him.

"Would you like some tea?" Avis asked.

"That would be nice," Wesley said, hoping that she would be gone long enough for him to talk to her husband alone.

"Charley...?"

"Yes, thank you," Charley answered his wife, though his dark eyes never left Wesley's. "You got something to say, Wesley?" he asked as soon as Avis left for the kitchen.

The directness threw Wesley for a moment, then he swallowed down his nerves and decided that it was probably better this way. "I wanted to talk about Ashton," he began, forcing his voice not to waver. "We've been seeing something of each other over the past few months and we feel that it has developed into something more serious."

He longed to move, to stand, to do something, but Wesley forced himself to remain seated and still. "I earn a decent income from the farm, have a large enough home to turn some of it into our own private quarters, so I can offer Ashton a good future," Wesley told the big man opposite him with no little pride. "But I'm here to ask your permission to propose marriage to your daughter. I'll respect your answer either way."

Avis stood with the tray of tea just outside the sitting room door and prayed that her husband wouldn't go back on the words she'd extracted from him the previous evening.

She almost dropped the tray when she heard her husband ask, "Have you had sex with my daughter?"

But Wesley didn't flinch, didn't lower his gaze from the man he hoped would one day be his father-in-law. "No. I respect your daughter in every way, I also love her more than I can say. If you can find it in you to give us your blessing, I can promise you…I shall spend the rest of my life trying to make her happy."

Charley slapped a large hand on his knee then said, "What kind of foolish nonsense is that! Ashton needs a firm hand – she'll have you wrapped around her little finger in a heartbeat if she thinks you'll let her!" Then Charley let out a low chuckle, "I just hope you know what you're taking on – life will never be dull while Ashton is around."

Standing to take the hand being held out to him, Wesley shook it with a relieved smile. "Thank you, Mr Langdon, Mrs Langdon," he added when Avis entered the room. "I can't tell you how happy this makes me."

Putting the tea tray on the coffee table, Avis reached up to give Wesley a hug.

He bent his tall frame to accept the hug and returned it gently.

"Welcome to the family, Wesley," Avis smiled, her eyes damp with happy tears.

"I think you're getting a little old to still be calling us Mr and Mrs Langdon," Charley told Wes as he retook his seat. "Charley and Avis will do fine."

Taking the tea that Avis had poured for him, Wesley grinned. "You've been Avis and Charley in my head for years – I was always worried it would slip out one day."

After the tea, Wesley was given a tour of the cottage and its gardens, then he drove to the Langdon Farm house in search of Ashton.

"Hey gorgeous," he called out when he saw Ashton emerge from the tack room, then smiled at Fenella when she followed Ashton out. "You girls going riding?"

"We just came back," Ashton informed him. "Fenella just wanted to hang a while."

"We could all go back to our house – I know Fallon is home and would like to see you both," Wesley suggested.

Fenella looked to Ashton for a decision – she still wasn't sure of herself though the trouble involving her father did seem to be less of a hot topic in the village.

"Sounds good – shall we?" Ashton asked Fenella.

"I'd like to see Fallon – we haven't had a chance to meet up in a while," Fenella agreed.

"Ok then – your carriage awaits," Wes smiled and gave them a comic bow.

"You idiot," Ashton giggled as they moved past him and Wesley grabbed her round the waist.

Watching the couple so happy together, Fenella wondered if she would ever know the same happiness in her own life.

"Morning," Jackson greeted the happy trio, his smile lingering on Fenella before continuing on his way.

Feeling a tingle down her spine, Fenella couldn't help looking over her shoulder at Jackson and was embarrassed to see him looking back at her.

He doffed an imaginary cap at her then turned into the stable yard and disappeared from view.

"I think he likes you," Ashton told her friend, noting the other woman's flushed cheeks.

"He's a single male – he probably looks at anything in a skirt," Fenella flicked off the observation with apparent ease.

"Maybe…" Ashton conceded, her smile curious, "…but he's never looked at me like that."

She felt Wesley's arm tighten about her waist. "And he'd better not or I'll have something to say about it!"

But the comment gave Fenella pause for thought. Would she be interested in Jackson if he made a move on her? He was certainly good looking, and he had a great body – but her father would never approve.

"You're just trying to fix me up," Fenella laughed it off. "He's probably got someone in the village anyway."

"Not that I know about," Wesley told her, unlocking his car and climbing in behind the wheel. He waited for the girls to climb in and do up their seatbelts, then took off for home.

When his sister saw who he'd brought home with him, Fallon gave Wesley a big grin.

"You two, with me," Fallon ordered, giving her brother a wink. "Mum's in the kitchen – I need help with an outfit and some girl talk."

Giving Ashton a resigned shrug, Wes went into the kitchen and got a welcoming smile from his mother.

"I brought Ashton and Fenella back with me, but Fallon has shanghaied them upstairs," he told his mother.

"I don't know what is going on with Fallon but she's been buzzing about all morning." Mrs Craemer shook her head then turned back to the sink where she filled the kettle to make tea.

"Is she seeing someone – she said she needed help with an outfit and some girl talk?"

"I'm not sure you could call it seeing someone – but Fallon did tell me that Carl Harrison had asked her out to dinner on Friday," Mrs Craemer smiled at her son. "I think it will do her good to move on – it doesn't seem like anything will come of her and Chad."

"What a pair!" Wesley blew out an exasperated breath and shook his head. "It's obvious they still care a lot about each other – but neither one of them will talk about what happened to break them up."

"Sometimes it goes too deep," his mother told Wesley wisely. "And sometimes it just hurts too much to put into words. Either way, Fallon seems to be getting over it - I hope Chad can move on too."

Wes didn't know if his mother was right, but he hadn't seen Chad so much as look at another woman since his sister. He just didn't seem to see them.

"I went to see Charles Langdon this morning," Wes announced, changing the subject. "I asked for his permission to propose to Ashton."

Wiping her hands on a tea-towel, Mrs Craemer stopped the busy work she was taking care of and turned to look at her son. "And what did he say?"

His smile was answer enough but Wesley said, "He gave us his blessing – they both did."

"Oh, this is wonderful," his mother hugged the tea-towel to her chest and beamed at Wesley. "So did you propose?"

But he shook his head, the smile still bright on Wesley's face. "I have the ring – bought it a while ago – but I want to wait for the right moment. You know...make it special."

CHAPTER NINETEEN

Before she knew it, Ashton was packing to go back to the academy. Wesley was going to drive her and Fonteyn back, so at least they would have that time too.

But she still felt unbelievably sad when it came time to say goodbye to the farm and her family.

"Take care, darling," her mother hugged her tightly. "And go out there and get another trophy – you're riding Fonteyn this time, aren't you?"

She had told them that she had a competition coming up, but Ashton hadn't told them what a big deal it was. She didn't want them to feel they had to come to watch her just because they were back home now.

"I am," Ashton grinned, pleased to think that she and her best friend would be competing together again. Fonteyn had always been more than just a horse to

Ashton, they had been together for a long time now. "We'll do our best to win – we always do."

"Just be careful," her dad warned, his large hand patting her shoulder. "I know you and your dare-devil ways, Ashton."

She looked up at her father and saw his raised brow.

"What, you don't think I'm aware of your hair-brained antics – parents know a lot more than they let on," her dad told her with a rueful smile.

"I love you, dad." And she surprised him by flinging her arms around his waist and hugging him tightly.

He returned her affection and stroked her head, her long red hair neatly plaited down her back.

"We're proud of you whatever you do, just bring yourself back home safely," he told her.

The journey was always a long one, but this time it felt interminable. Her heart was heavy and even Fonteyn had seemed reluctant to climb into the horsebox.

"Maybe I'm being selfish bringing Fonteyn home with me," Ashton observed out of the blue. "It's a lot of travelling, especially when we have competitions to get to as well."

"Are you saying you'd rather stay at the academy as you did before?" Wesley asked, not liking her subdued mood.

"No. Not at all." Ashton turned in her seat to look at Wesley in surprise. "I love coming home, seeing you and the rest of the family, and getting time to enjoy the farm again." She sighed heavily, glancing back at Fonteyn through the peep grill above their seats.

"But…?" Wesley asked warily.

Ashton shrugged, unable to put her feelings into words. "I don't know – I feel like crying yet I know I have nothing to cry about. I have no idea why I feel so sad."

Taking one hand off the wheel, Wes laid it over hers in her lap and gave them a gentle squeeze. "I'm not the least bit surprised you're feeling sad. Your parents have only just come home after being away for a whole year. It's only natural to want more time with them."

Turning a hand over, Ashton held his and tried to pull herself out of the silly mood. "At least I get you to myself for a while – we didn't get much of that this time."

"I told you what it would be like once everyone knew about us," he smiled. "But I'm glad we told them – it feels good to be accepted as a couple."

"I got Chad on side before mum and dad got home," she confided with a chuckle. "I asked him to side with me if it looked like dad was going to give us some grief."

Wesley's chuckle was deep and somewhat relieved. "That was probably a very good idea – I think your dad may have had a few reservations, but he seems to have accepted the situation."

He thought about the morning he'd gone to Charley to ask for his permission to propose marriage to his daughter. He'd never been so scared in all his life – scared of the man, scared of the answer he might give and that ultimate fear...that soul deep dread of losing the future he so badly wanted with Ashton.

She watched him, saw the flicker of emotions that played across his handsome face. "What's wrong?"

"What?"

"You looked a million miles away – lost in some bad thoughts," Ashton observed with a frown.

"No...not bad thoughts – just thoughts," Wes said evasively.

"Thoughts you don't want to share?"

"I was just thinking how much I'm going to miss you – it's been great seeing you every day." Wes smiled over at her, giving the hand he still held a gentle squeeze.

Not sure that she believed him entirely, Ashton didn't push the point but decided that her maudlin mood must have rubbed off on him and determined to shake it off.

"I bet Tony's got a whole lot of training lined up for me before the big competition," Ashton frowned, but smiled through it. "He's such a slave-driver. And he'll want me to work out on Vanquish as well as practice on Fonteyn."

"You love it," Wes chuckled, knowing how much she loved to compete. "You may well miss home, but you love the showjumping life too."

She had to admit, even just to herself, that the nearer they got to the academy the more her thoughts had moved to her life there and the work that would be expected of her. And she couldn't disagree, she did love the showjumping life...she just didn't like leaving home behind.

"Will you be coming to the competition," she asked, determined not to slide back into the doldrums.

"I'm staying," Wes replied, springing his surprise.

"What...I don't understand...you're staying where...when?"

He laughed, loving her excited babbling. "I'm staying for the whole week while you're down here. I've already spoken to Tony, he's amenable to me coming with you to Birmingham – I've booked into the little hotel I usually stay in," he smiled, delighted that he'd managed to stun her speechless.

If it weren't for the damn seat belt, she'd have flung herself at him and never let go. "I love you, Wes. I really do love you."

When she started to sniff and wipe tears away, he turned to look at her. "And that makes you cry?"

"No, you idiot – I'm crying because I'm happy. Very, very happy."

She was right about the training schedule Tony had waiting for her. It started an hour after they'd got Fonteyn settled.

Vanquish was being his usual taciturn self, kicking up his back legs and doing just as he pleased. But Ashton was an excellent rider, she gave him some leeway for the first few minutes then firmly brought him into line.

She took him for their usual couple of laps around the paddock before attempting any of the jumps. It served to settle him and they found their rhythm.

The first round over the jumps was taken slowly, concentrating on not getting any of them down. Ashton looked to Tony and he signalled that he was timing the next one, just as if she was against the clock in a real competition.

The moment she approached the first fence Tony started his stopwatch and they were away.

Vanquish seemed to know that this round was different, sensed his rider's demands and cooperated fully.

They flew over fences, turned sharply and balanced

perfectly – their rhythm was faultless. It was amazing – after three weeks away Ashton had expected things to be a bit sticky for a while, but Vanquish was incredible.

Her grin was bright and wide as she rode up to Tony and Wesley. "Did you see that – he was brilliant?!"

"You both were," Wesley told her.

"Not bad," Tony nodded, then smiled when Ashton's own smile faltered. "Ok, pretty good."

Still sat atop the horse, Ashton leaned forward and gave Vanquish a congratulatory pat and stroked his neck. "Don't listen to him – we were brilliant!"

Now Tony laughed and rolled his eyes to Wesley. "Getting a bit full of herself – I don't know how you put up with it. There'll be no living with her if she wins at Birmingham – you know that don't you."

Grinning with pride Wesley looked up at Ashton, eyes shining bright with love. "That's my girl!"

"Too right!" Ashton declared, then turned Vanquish to take another run at the circuit of jumps.

The next few days were indeed tough, even gruelling, but Ashton was determined to succeed and knew having Tony as her coach was the best advantage she could get.

Even when he criticised her style, shouted at her to get her head in the game or simply stood stiff and frowning at her from the side of the paddock, Ashton took it all in her stride and tried to learn from the best.

And that's what Tony had been, in his day. Until the injury that had shattered his career, her coach had been number 1 in the world of showjumping, and had been in the top 5 for most of his illustrious career.

Not only was she a much better rider since taking instruction from Tony, but Fonteyn had come on too. She had always been responsive, trusting her rider to know what she was doing. But now Fonteyn was correcting her stride more easily, preparing for the jumps and taking them in style.

Ashton couldn't wait to take her to Birmingham, to feel the elation she got with no other horse as they competed together.

"I'm taking you out tonight," Wesley announced the night before the big event. "I'll have you back early – I know you'll want to get to bed, we've got an early start tomorrow."

"Thanks. It'll be nice to wind down for a bit, but I will need that early night."

"No probs. I'll pick you up at 7."

For once there was no one around and Wesley took full advantage. Moving in for a kiss, he pulled her to him and rubbed his hands up and down her spine, allowing them to move lower and cup her bottom.

"Wesley!"

"Hush." His lips were gentle, one hand stayed on her bottom the other moved to the nape of her neck and held her. The kiss moved deeper, and she felt the hard length of him between them.

When Wesley used the hand on her bottom to pull her in closer, Ashton didn't resist but squirmed against him and groaned into his mouth.

"Jesus…if we weren't in the middle of a damn field I might just take you right this minute."

Her eyes were full of heat when Ashton looked up at him, her smile nothing less than inviting. "About bloody time! Do I take it we're ready to take it to the next level?"

"So eager," he chuckled, dipping his head to taste her ruby lips again. But when he raised it to look at her again, his eyes were intense, his voice deep with wanting. "I need you, Ashton. I want you, sure…have wanted you since you were 16. But I need to feel you in my arms and know it's where you're always going to be − that it's where you will always want to be."

"I will. There's nowhere else for me. No one else for me. I've known that since I was 16 too − you just took a bit longer to realise it."

When their lips met this time, it formed a seal on their promises. They were ready to commit to each other completely, to join their minds bodies and souls in the ultimate act of love.

When he pulled back, Wesley had to take a deep breath and let it out slowly to steady himself. "I will not take you in a bloody field for your first time. I want to make it special...for both of us."

He'd imagined the moment many times, how he'd love her, touch her in ways that would bring her the most pleasure. And he would enjoy finding out what she liked, what made her moan and writhe then doing it again and again until she screamed for him.

And then he would fill her, would feel her heat surround him and know that this is where he belonged. Joined, they would take each other on a journey that could never be repeated — their first time would be memorable, he would make sure of that.

CHAPTER TWENTY

Up earlier than usual, Ashton spent a lot of time with Fonteyn. She mucked out her stable, gave the mare fresh hay and water then began the grooming process.

"Today could be the decider for us. If we win there's no way for anyone to take the championship away from us — there just aren't enough points in the few competitions left to allow anyone to catch up to us," Ashton crooned softly, all the time stroking the brush over Fonteyn's coat.

"But that's only if we win — second place could leave a tie open, but we're not going to give them that…right?"

The Birmingham show was always a big one, a major event on the Equestrienne Academy calendar. In years past, the winner of this event had gone on to take the league championship, and Ashton didn't want to disappoint.

Wes was a regular visitor to the academy and no one challenged him when he made his way over to the stable block. "You need a hand with anything?"

Hand flying to her heart to still it, Ashton turned panicked eyes to him. "Christ, you almost gave me a heart attack!"

But a smile quickly bloomed and Wes knew he was forgiven for making her jump. "Sorry. I thought you'd get an early start so I thought I'd come over and give you a hand, though it looks like you've done it all."

"You can start braiding Fonteyn's mane," Ashton suggested. "Leave a couple of inches loose then twist the plait to form a knot and pull the long end through – they'll form fancy tufts down the back of her neck."

"What do you want doing with the forelock?"

Nothing, just leave that loose," Ashton instructed. "You're going to look beautiful – your coat has a lovely shine to it."

Fonteyn stood patiently, allowed herself to be fussed and fancied up without so much as a stomp of an ill-tempered hoof.

"I won't oil her hooves yet – I'll do that when we get to Birmingham so they stay looking nice for the competition," Ashton smiled up at Wes.

"And what about you – are you going to get all fancied up for this meet?"

"I most certainly am," Ashton said with pride. "Fonteyn will always steal the show but I'll make an effort so I don't show her up."

"You always look spot on when you compete," Wes told her approvingly. "You both do."

The journey was long but not at all tedious. Wes and Tony found they had a lot in common and Tony was interested in the fact that Wes used to compete.

"So why did you give it up – sounds like you could have had a promising career," Tony observed.

"Titan is a good horse, no doubt about that," Wes told him. "But I have a farm to run – not as big as Langdon Farm, but it still takes a lot of looking after."

Tony nodded understandingly.

"I don't know how you manage it all – without your dad all the heavy stuff falls to you now," Ashton observed.

"Fallon helps out where she can – but you're right, I will need to get some help in soon."

Wondering why he hadn't done so before this, Ashton decided not to ask. Wes had been devastated when his dad had died from an aggressive form of cancer. One minute he was diagnosed, the next he was gone.

"I've loaned Jackson a few times when I've really needed to – Matt's been great about it," Wes told them. "He does what he needs to on your farm first, then I pay him extra to help out on mine."

"I know Jackson's saving up for a place of his own, so that must suit him down to the ground," Ashton remarked.

"He's a hard worker, but I will need someone else – maybe a good part-timer after Christmas," Wes said, considering his options.

Ashton smiled like she'd got a secret she was dying to tell but hesitated to do so.

"What?" Wes asked when he caught the look.

She shifted in her seat and even felt her cheeks heat, but decided she couldn't resist a good gossip. "I think Jackson's got the hots for Fenella."

Shaking his head, Wes gave a low chuckle and looked at Ashton like she'd lost her mind. "Not on your life! Jackson's not stupid enough to get involved with Swain's daughter – he just isn't."

"Swain...are you talking about Theodore Swain, the newspaper chappy?" Tony asked, not usually given to getting involved in such talk.

"That's right." Wes turned curious eyes to Tony and was surprised to see anger that the coach hadn't been quick enough to hide. "You know him?"

Through compressed lips, Tony said, "Of him, more like. Showjumping is full of big money men and Swain was throwing his weight around a few years back – tried to muscle in on a couple of the more prestigious committees – didn't like it when they slammed the door in his face!"

"Jesus, that was either a very brave or a very stupid thing to do," Wes commented, whistling out a breath.

"So, you know all about him – his dodgy background and his underhanded way of doing business?" Tony asked.

"I don't know much, but rumour has it good old Theo didn't make his millions without breaking a few rules. Maybe even a few necks," Wes added, thinking about a few things Chad had told him. His best friend had done some deep research for his books and had unearthed a great deal of dirt on the newspaper mogul.

A lot had been hearsay, but Chad had spoken to a few people who claimed to have dealt with Swain personally – had felt his wrath and deemed themselves lucky to still be alive.

"According to some sources, the newspaper business was built on a lot of shady dealings and continues to be used to put a respectable front on Swain's continued underground activities," Wes added, and thought those committee men probably wouldn't have been so quick to slam that door in Swain's face if they'd been fully aware of what the man was capable of.

Tony looked like he was giving Wesley's words a lot of

thought. "There was nothing that we could prove but, Michael Trader, one of the more vocal opposers to Swain, died in a car accident only days after the decision to block Swain was made. We all thought it was ominous timing," Tony sighed heavily.

"Hell's teeth!" Ashton exclaimed.

"Oh yes, and then some," Tony sighed again. "You should keep as far away from that man as possible – I didn't realise he lived in your area."

"We don't see much of him now, but his wife and daughter still live on the old farm that he transformed," Ashton informed him. "There was a lot of trouble over Swain wanting my brother, Matt, to marry his daughter, Fenella – my brother ended up in gaol accused of murder."

"Good grief! That man is a bloody despot – if he can't get his own way he just stomps all over people's lives until they either give in or die trying to stand up to him!"

On arriving at the showground, Tony pulled the horsebox into their allotted space and began all the usual preparations.

Wes stayed with Fonteyn while Tony and Ashton took a walk around the course discussing, as they always did, tactics and a few words of wisdom from the experienced coach.

By the time they got back, Wes had phoned his mother and been told that Jackson and Matt had everything under control. The two men had been treated to a hot lunch the day before and she was preparing another meal for today.

His mother loved cooking and nothing pleased her more than men with good appetites.

"How is it?" Wes asked when Tony and Ashton reached him.

"The ground is a bit heavy in places – they've had a few storms over the last couple of weeks – but I think Fonteyn will handle it," Tony nodded, obviously satisfied.

"Some of those jumps are enormous," Ashton observed with a frown. "But if any horse can pull it out of the bag, Fonteyn can!"

"Are you nervous?" Wesley asked, and Tony looked at Ashton, interested in her answer.

"Of course I'm nervous – I'm not an idiot!"

Chuckling softly, Tony raised a brow at Wesley and said, "The girl is just sweetness and light, isn't she – a delicate English rose...just watch out for those thorns!"

Ashton had the grace to blush but stood her ground. "Just because I call a spade a spade doesn't mean I'm a bloody shrew! I just meant..." she hesitated, drew in a breath then let it out slowly. "I just meant, I'm not stupid enough to take any competition for granted. Nerves are good, they get the adrenaline pumping, but when it comes right down to it, Fonteyn and I are up to the job. That's the one thing I never doubt."

She was sixth in the line-up, and Ashton took the opportunity to watch how a few of her competitors dealt with the course.

"She's good..." Wes commented at Ashton's side, "...and the horse is fearless. I see what you meant about some of those jumps, though."

A moment later and a pole fell, giving the rider 4 points against her. This round wasn't against the clock and the rider steadied her horse to make sure of a clear round from then on.

"This is a tough one – I wouldn't be surprised if no one gets a clear round," Ashton commented after another rider got exactly the same fence down.

But the next rider cleared it, continued with studied care and managed to finish with a clear round, much to the audiences delight.

"I'd better get ready," Ashton told Wes, and they both turned to go back to the horsebox.

By the time Ashton got Fonteyn to the competition ring, the previous rider was half way through the course.

Horse and rider cleared the seemingly jinxed fence and looked like doing well. But a too sharp turn didn't allow the horse to line itself up properly for the double and the horse stopped abruptly.

Ashton watched in horror as the rider was catapulted over the horse's head, landed on the wide spread and was buried in the debris of broken poles and their holders.

The longer it took for the rider to get to their feet, the more the possibility of serious injury buzzed through the ground.

Eventually a stretcher was brought on and Ashton looked down at Tony.

"Stop worrying," he told her. "It's probably just a precaution. Take Fonteyn over a couple of the practice jumps and keep your mind on what we talked about."

Doing as she was told, Ashton took Fonteyn around the small warm up ring and eventually took the practice jumps, feeling better once she had.

You've seen people fall before, you know it happens. Just concentrate on not doing the same thing – follow the game plan and everything will be alright!

But she had an ominous feeling in her gut, not something she had ever experienced before a competition. It wasn't nerves and it wasn't fear – Ashton couldn't put her finger on exactly what it was, but it gnawed at her insides.

She saw Tony wave to her, heard the Tannoy announce her and Fonteyn as the next competitors and assumed the course had been rebuilt.

"Just keep your mind on what you're doing and you'll be fine." Tony advised as she passed him.

The knowledgeable crowd applauded her entrance, and Ashton looked around for Wesley. He'd managed to get a standing position to the left side of the starting position and gave her an encouraging smile.

Readying herself, Ashton leaned forward and whispered, "Ready girl," and gave Fonteyn a pat on her neck before urging her on.

The first two fences were warm ups, high but not as high as the rest of the fences. Fonteyn was graceful in her efforts and Ashton soon forgot the tragic scene of moments ago. Her spirit lifted as they flew over fences and took some tight turns with ease – she didn't push Fonteyn for speed, this round wasn't against the clock.

A double spread that Ashton had thought challenging when walking the course with Tony, now looked doable from the lofty height of Fonteyn's back and they glided over the two fences easily.

The next was the problem fence, one that three riders so far had knocked the top pole off of.

She steadied, lined Fonteyn up and cleared it with inches to spare and Ashton smiled for the first time.

With growing confidence, Ashton and Fonteyn went on to achieve a clear round and the audience went wild.

She was a favourite on the competition circuit – Ashton couldn't understand it, but the regulars in the audience seemed to have taken her into their hearts.

Beaming at Tony, Ashton slid out of the saddle and was drawn into a congratulatory hug by her coach.

"That was well done," Tony smiled, taking Fonteyn's reins and giving the mare an affectionate pat. "That goes for you too."

"I felt much better when we got passed the jinxed fence – it was like a weight lifting off me," Ashton sighed.

"Don't let the idea of jinxes take hold – they're all just fences, some of them more difficult than others," Tony told her. "You handled yourself well out there."

By the time they got back to the horsebox, Wesley was already there.

"You were brilliant," he grinned, scooping Ashton up to swing her around.

She laughed, loving that he was here and that he was obviously enjoying her success.

"I bet you held your breath when I came to that spread – the one so many people got down," Ashton clarified unnecessarily.

"I have to admit, it gave my heart a few flutters but I knew my girl could do it."

"You did?" Her head tilted and she looked dubious.

"I most certainly did!" Wes confirmed with a kiss.

CHAPTER TWENTY-ONE

She was so happy, life just didn't get much better than this, did it?

On the verge of making a solid statement in the world of showjumping, Ashton was on an all-time high.

So what if she had to spend a week at the academy a month, and do the odd competition in between, she had Wesley on her side and even encouraging her to grab the brass ring while it was within reach.

How many women could say such a thing, could honestly claim that their man was behind their dreams 100%.

It wasn't about owning her, not for Wesley. Hell, he'd only just come round to the idea of them becoming honest to goodness lovers – and that was a wonder to Ashton.

She'd seen him with a lot of women over the last few years, had been jealous as hell when he'd overtly flirted with them, making his intention to bed them obvious.

It had been a painful time for her.

But now he was hers. Wesley had declared himself in love with her and made every effort to spend as much time with her as possible.

Yes, life was very, very good.

The first round had been tough, but the second was tougher still. The wall had been raised and so had a couple of the other, trickier jumps.

Again, Ashton stood at the opening between the warmup ring and the competition ring watching the first couple of rider's progress.

The first got a clear round, but it had been a near thing – a brick in the wall had teetered on the edge of falling but had miraculously remained in place.

The next had two fences down and a brick off the wall – Josh was out of the competition. She hadn't seen him in a while and Ashton felt sad that he'd gone out.

They may not be kissing buddies any more, but she was still very fond of Josh.

She ran back to the horsebox, got up on Fonteyn and worked on relaxing her breathing. Tony gave more words of inspiration and encouragement then she rode Fonteyn round to await their turn.

Settling herself, Ashton focused on the task in hand and barely heard the crowd congratulating the last rider on her clear round.

The Tannoy announced her entrance and Ashton pulled on the strength that confidence and determination gave her. She was riding a horse who would give her everything, and she would demand it all now.

Again she moved with care, not forcing the pace as this second round was still not against the clock. The main aim was to get a clear round and they were half way through when Fonteyn's back hooves clipped a pole.

A nervous look back told Ashton that it had rattled but stayed in place, and it was on to the next fence.

The wall loomed large, larger than Ashton had ever attempted in a competition – but this was the big leagues and all the riders were being tested.

Her heart swelled as Fonteyn took her safely over it, and then a double that had a tricky turn to follow.

She was coming up to a difficult triple; you could have heard a pin drop, the silence was so complete.

Her heart beat loud in her ears, Fonteyn's hoof beats keeping time – they were over the first fence, then the second and third were cleared cleanly.

Just two more fences and they would be home free – through to the last and final round.

The crowd roared its appreciation and Ashton finally let the sound in. It was overwhelming and she turned to wave before exiting the ring and dismounting.

"Oh my god...that was so amazing," she cried as Tony put an arm across her shoulders and beamed his delight.

"That it was," Tony smiled. "But don't lose your focus, you still have to jump against the clock and that will need all your concentration."

Acknowledging the congratulations of well-wishers, Ashton walked Fonteyn back to the horsebox and found Wesley there to greet her.

Tony took Fonteyn and left the couple to enjoy the moment. He didn't mind Wesley being around, now that he knew the young man was all for Ashton's chosen career — and, although he no longer competed, his knowledge of showjumping didn't hurt either.

"Christ, that was nerve-racking," Wesley told her, holding Ashton tightly against him. "I'll go grey before I'm 30 at this rate."

"I don't care, I'll love you anyway," Ashton laughed.

"You'd better. I plan to love you till we're both old and grey — I'm looking forward to a life with you in it."

"You're all gooey and smoochy," Ashton chuckled, but didn't resist when his lips claimed hers again.

"I don't care what you call it, I love you with everything I am, I always will."

And then he realised – what better moment would there be to propose to the woman he wanted to spend the rest of his life with.

Suddenly he was on one knee, careless of the damp grass and the people who had stopped milling around but now stood watching as he took a small box from his jeans pocket and held it out to her with both hands.

"Ashton Langdon, would you do me the very great honour of making me the happiest man alive. Will you let me love you and care for you always to the end of our days - I'm asking you…no…I'm begging you…please, would you be my wife."

As he spoke the last words, Wesley opened the small box to reveal a gold ring with three diamonds in a row atop it.

Ashton looked taken aback, lost for words, and the crowd held its collective breath.

Then she felt tears stinging her eyes and her heart leapt with joy. "Yes. Of course, yes."

The crowd cheered, and even Tony grinned at the happy couple.

Taking the ring out of the box, Wesley slipped it onto the second finger of her left hand then kissed Ashton with a passion that blocked out everything and everyone around them.

"Uh-hum," Tony coughed discreetly when it didn't appear like they'd be coming up for air any time soon. "You need to get Fonteyn round to the warm up ring – you'll be up in a few minutes."

Blushing like a schoolgirl, Ashton didn't think she could contain her happiness and shot her left hand out for Tony to inspect.

"Very nice…I hope you'll both be very happy…but…"

"Ok, ok, I'm going," Ashton told him, but her grin just wouldn't be dimmed. "I'm going to win this competition for us," she told Wesley after mounting Fonteyn. "It will be a wonderful day to remember."

"Concentrate, Ashton," Tony warned, but he doubted she really heard him.

Cantering Fonteyn round the warm up ring, Ashton didn't bother to take the jumps but just settled herself down with an almighty effort of will.

"We can do this, girl," she told the mare. "We can go all the way to the top – you and me against the best in the world."

The Tannoy announced her and Ashton rode Fonteyn into the ring for the final round. The crowd greeted them enthusiastically but hushed quickly, anxious for the round to begin.

The signal came and they were off, taking the first

jump easily then chancing a tight turn to shave vital seconds off the time and then flew over the second.

Wesley was so tense he was clenching his fists, his nails biting into his palms without notice.

Come on...come on...oh Christ! Yes, that's it...keep going... He was a nervous wreck, taking each jump with her as Ashton rounded to take the wall.

She took only a millisecond to line Fonteyn up and the mare charged the fence, taking off as if she might soar into the heavens.

The crowd applauded briefly, silent again as Ashton began the triple, one fence then two then three were jumped and cleared in quick succession.

Just two more fences to go.

They took the turn sharper than any other rider, Fonteyn's balance unbelievable and Ashton's fearless determination gleaming in her eyes.

Wesley recognised that look, had seen it so many times over the years as they had shared their childhood. Now he watched as the fierce woman he loved cleared the last fence and listened as the crowd went absolutely wild.

They had shaved a full second off the best time, and that had been a seriously good effort.

Ashton looked dazed and then elated, returning the

crowd's wave before exiting the ring.

Leaning forward on Fonteyn's neck, she stroked the mare and thanked her for a stupendous effort. "You never give less than everything," she crooned softly, tears running down her cheeks unnoticed. "You're the very best friend I could ever have."

She had said those same words when she was 12 after her dad had presented her with the yearling and declared that she was entirely responsible for its care.

They had bonded from the first, Ashton had even slept in the mare's stall when she'd gotten ill with colic. Nothing her parents said could convince the young Ashton to leave her friend to suffer alone.

Now they were climbing the ladder of success together, a partnership meant for even bigger and better things.

There were two more riders to go, which gave Ashton just enough time to clean herself up.

Wesley dashed back to congratulate her, so excited he kept lifting her in the air and twirling her around.

"She'll get sick and dizzy if you don't put her down," Tony remonstrated, but his smile remained warm.

"And I need to clean up – I can't believe I burst into tears, anyone would think I'd lost," Ashton chuckled at her own idiocy.

"You look great, and so do you," Wesley told Fonteyn, stroking the mare's neck repeatedly.

Ashton had just wiped her face and tidied her hair when the Tannoy voice asked for the top four riders to re-enter the ring for the presentation.

Boosting her up into Fonteyn's saddle, Wesley said, "I'm so proud of you – we'll make our way round for the presentation. I love you, Ashton."

She could only nod, her eyes were already filling up again and her throat was working hard to swallow back the emotions that were swamping her.

Turning Fonteyn, Ashton made her way to the competition ring and entered to rousing applause from the enthusiastic crowd.

The announcements were made, speeches given and the presentation itself began.

One by one the riders were announced in reverse order until only Ashton and Fonteyn were left.

As soon as their names were given as the winners the applause trebled and Ashton felt her heart fill with pride. It took quite a while for the noise to abate enough to allow the officials to continue with the presentation.

Ashton watched as the VIP approached them, then felt something happening that didn't make any sense and the crowd were screaming now, but in shock instead of elation.

Fonteyn had crumpled beneath her, going down heavily onto her knees and then falling with a distressing thud to her side.

Ashton had moved instinctively, her right foot moving out of the stirrup to whip her leg over Fonteyn's back. But the second she got to her feet, Ashton moved forward to the mare's head and was inconsolable as the reality of the situation hit.

But how could this be happening, only minutes ago they had been flying over fences, dodging and weaving between them in a familiar dance. Fonteyn had been brilliant, full of life and raring to go – Fonteyn and Ashton, Ashton and Fonteyn, you didn't say one name without saying the other – they were one in every way that counted.

Bending over Fonteyn, Ashton stroked her head and laid her wet cheek against the mare. "Don't leave me…please don't leave me. You're my best friend in all the world…my…my…best friend…"

The tears and sobs racked Ashton violently as she shrugged off the attempts of people nearby to move her away from the dead horse.

Then Wesley was there – he didn't try to force her away but knelt beside her to stroke the still warm horse.

"She loved you, Ashton. Fonteyn gave you everything

she had and she died a winner." When his arm went around her shoulders, Ashton finally turned away from Fonteyn and into Wesley, her heart broken to pieces.

An announcement was made and the event was closed with a few words that extolled Fonteyn's big heart and valiant spirit.

It was all so much noise to Ashton – none of the words sank in, not the praise being heaped on the special partnership she had shared with Fonteyn, not the pats on the shoulder and people wishing her well – the nightmare just wouldn't end.

Fonteyn was still dead no matter what anyone said or did, but Ashton couldn't seem to take it in.

She was sat in the cab of the horsebox with Wesley when her sobs finally eased through physical exhaustion, moments later she fell into a deep dark and thankfully dreamless sleep.

CHAPTER TWENTY-TWO

Wesley had insisted that Ashton would stay with him at the hotel that night, he wouldn't risk her waking in the night alone, and she had gone with him willingly.

It never occurred to him to take advantage of the situation, he wanted only to hold her and to soothe the terrible pain in her heart.

It had been tragic, unbelievably heartbreakingly tragic, to see what should have been a glorious and memorable moment turn into an unspeakably sad catastrophe of loss.

She was restless in the night, but never turned away from Wesley. Clinging to his warmth and strength seemed to be instinctual and he was glad that he had insisted she stay with him.

As dawn was breaking her lovely eyes opened and Wesley looked deep into the sadness that still haunted them.

Putting a gentle hand to her cheek Wes smiled wanly. "I know your heart must be hurting badly, but I want you to know that I'm here for you and I'll be here for you for as long as you need me to stay."

For the longest moment, Ashton just looked and blinked back the immediate tears. "Take me home, Wesley. I really need to go home."

Her voice was so tiny and pitiful and it never occurred to Wesley to deny her wish. "We'll go right after breakfast. I'll call Tony to explain that you need some time at home. He'll understand, I'm sure."

But she was already shaking her head. "No, I want to go home for good – there's nothing here for me now."

He frowned, then decided that she would have plenty of time to think later. Ashton was probably still in shock and shouldn't be making decisions that would impact her life right now.

"Don't think of it now, Ashton. I'll take you home and you can just forget all about the academy for now – or you can forget about it all together. Whatever you decide I'll back you all the way."

He moved forward, her lips were just an inch away and Wesley needed to kiss them, to feel that intimate touch that said, 'it's ok I'm right here'.

But Ashton didn't want that brief touch, didn't want

him to move away and leave her bleeding. She reached across, put her hand to the nape of his neck and held Wes to her as she deepened the kiss, desperate to feel something other than the deep pain that was twisting in her heart.

Pulling her to him, Wesley meant only to offer comfort, to put his arms around the woman he loved and give her all the strength he could will into her. But that wasn't enough – wasn't nearly enough for Ashton.

"I need you, Wes – I need to be a part of you, I need you to be a part of me – don't leave me separate and alone."

He loved her and Ashton's plea almost broke his heart. But this would be her first time, he wasn't sure that it would be appropriate and hated to think that he might be taking advantage of her.

"Ashton, you don't know what you're asking-"

But she cut his protest off with a kiss, covering his mouth and swallowing the words that might have denied her the very thing she needed…Wesley.

He took it slow, caressed her body so gently almost afraid she would break beneath his touch. But instead she came alive, moaned for him, begged for more and opened to him eagerly when he finally moved over her.

"Ashton…?"

A moment of hesitation, one last chance for her to change her mind, but Ashton would have none of it.

"Inside me, please Wesley. Make me yours completely…I don't want to be alone."

Reaching for his jeans, Wesley took a silver foil packet out of a pocket and made sure that Ashton was safe.

Kissing a tear away, Wesley lowered himself and entered her as slowly and gently as he was able then stayed completely still.

"Are you alright?" he asked, afraid that he had hurt her.

"Yes…it only hurt for a moment, but it's gone now, I think."

He began to move, just small slow strokes to allow her to accept him, to give her tight body time to relax around him.

When her hand moved to his buttocks, pulling him to her as she raised her hips, Wesley took it as a signal that she wanted more.

Still he was careful, gradually increasing the depth and speed of his lovemaking. It was a miracle - to feel her response, to feel everything he had ever wanted come together in this precious moment was nothing less than a miracle.

"I love you, Ashton. I've always loved you and I always will."

She was flying, her body rippling with the pleasures he gave to her, and Ashton opened herself up to him completely.

Trusting Wes to take care of her, knowing that he had wanted this moment to be a commitment, a sealing of their promises to a life together, only made Ashton love and want him more.

And she needed him now. Her heart was hurting and Wesley would make her forget, even just for a little while.

"You're my life, Wesley. I want to be with you always."

Her hand on his cheek, their eyes locked and filled with a love that couldn't be put into mere words, they flew over the edge of passion together, falling into each other in a coming home that was long awaited.

Wesley had already changed the hotel booking to include Ashton the night before, so she was welcomed at the breakfast table by a smiling waitress.

"Mr Craemer ordered a full English breakfast for you...," the waitress told Ashton, holding her pad and pencil at the ready, "...but if you'd like anything different...?"

"No, that will be fine," Ashton told the young woman, who went off to confirm the order.

"Just eat what you feel like," Wes encouraged. "Want some tea?"

Ashton couldn't resist the smile that tugged at her reluctant lips. "Listen to us, we already sound like a married couple."

Pleased that she could see some humour in the situation, Wesley played up to it. "You're mine, now – a wedding is just a formality. An important one, I'll grant you, but what we are to each other is even more important."

Her smile widened and Ashton covered his hand with her own. "I couldn't agree more. I am yours, and you are mine – we're as married in our hearts as we will be in law when the time is right."

It was precious, this time of joining bodies, hearts and minds. This moment could never be repeated in exactly the same way, so they savoured it, kept the memory of their first time together as a beloved secret.

The journey back to Langdon Farm was not as carefree as the journey down to the academy had been. The horsebox was empty and Ashton had to force herself not to look back through the hatch where she would have been able to see Fonteyn, had she still been alive.

The weight in her heart was heavy and painful, but Ashton had stopped crying and determined not to allow any more tears to fall. There would be time for that when she was back home, when Fonteyn's loss would become a reality that couldn't be denied.

Gone…her best friend in all the world was gone. They'd had such wonderful times together, she remembered. Fonteyn had been a spindly yearling when her father had presented Ashton with her.

The way she'd pranced about the field had given Ashton the idea for her name – Fonteyn, the surname of the most brilliant ballet dancer of all time, Margot Fonteyn, and a particular favourite of the young Ashton.

They had made such memories together, the hours of training and fun that had united the two young spirits. Fonteyn had always been courageous, taking to jumping barrels and excelling at gymkhana mounted games.

Fonteyn's speed and agility had been noted very early on, and the bond between the pair had engendered a mutual trust that bordered on foolhardiness.

She would leave a huge gap in Ashton's life, but it would fill with the wonderful remembering's that time would enable eventually.

The first week of Ashton's return home had been difficult and the family had given her the space and time she needed to settle herself.

It had been extremely difficult the first time she had gone to the stables, had entered the stall that Fonteyn had regularly occupied.

"You shared something very special," Pam told her. "Don't let the pain of losing Fonteyn block out all the lovely memories you made together."

Eventually the pain did give way to a sadness that Ashton could bare, and Pam had been right, the memories were lovely and she began to recall them more and more as the days passed.

"Have you thought about going back to the academy?" Wesley asked as they sat by the river that ran through the Craemer farm.

Feeling Wesley's arms around her as she leaned back against him, Ashton marvelled at his generosity and smiled. "Showjumping is something I did because I loved doing it with Fonteyn – it was our accomplishment – it was just...ours," Ashton explained. "I don't need to go back to the academy when all that I want and love is right here."

If only he could believe that, but Wesley worried that Ashton would come to regret that decision and might also come to resent the life they made together.

"I want you to give it more thought – you have a good rapport with Vanquish to build on and I know Tony is hoping you'll go back."

Turning to look at him, Ashton frowned, confused and hurt by his insistence that she return to the academy. "Anyone would think you want me to go – that you don't want me around. Is that it, Wesley?" She turned more fully, watching his expression for confirmation of her fears. "Has the prospect of my being home all the time given you second thoughts about us?"

He shook his head but Wesley still looked unsure. "I don't have any second or third thoughts about us – our future together is signed and sealed. But I am worried that it won't be enough for you that life on a farm will be boring after what you've experienced."

Taking her hands with both of his, Wesley looked deep into her eyes to show Ashton that he was being sincere. "Nothing would make me happier than having you in my life for every single day of it, but I don't want you to come to regret giving up your chances or to resent the only life that I can give you."

Her smile took Wesley's breath away and her words wiped away all of his doubts. "Fonteyn was my best friend, doing what we did together, growing up together, was every young girl's dream. But I'm a woman now and, as such, I want what many women want – I want to get married to the man I love, to bear his children and take care of the home we'll build together." Taking his face between her hands, Ashton leaned in for a kiss. "In other words, I want you, Wesley – I always have."

*****

If you have enjoyed this book, please leave a review at the place of purchase.

Susan Elle